DL Inc.

K.G. Watson

Copyright © 2023 Ken Watson
Published by Pandamonium Publishing House
www.pandamoniumpublishing.com
All rights reserved. No part of this book may be reproduced or copied in any manner or stored in any retrieval system. Please contact the publisher for express written permission to use excerpts from this book in articles and media.
ISBN: 978-1-989506-76-9
This book is a work of fiction. Names, characters, businesses, organizations, places, events, and incidents either are products of the author's imagination or are used fictitiously. Any resemblance to actual persons living or dead, events, or locales are entirely coincidental.

CONTENTS

Chapter 1..pg 1
Chapter 2..pg 10
Chapter 3..pg 21
Chapter 4..pg 25
Chapter 5..pg 27
Chapter 6..pg 40
Chapter 7..pg 44
Chapter 8..pg 56
Chapter 9..pg 64
Chapter 10..pg 68
Chapter 11..pg 21
Chapter 12..pg 75
Chapter 13..pg 101
Chapter 14..pg 114
Chapter 15..pg 134
Chapter 16..pg 153
Chapter 17..pg 171
Chapter 18..pg 177

1

"All things change – well except death and taxes," they say. "Those of this vision make such caveats, with a superior chuckle, unaware of their myopia. The statement confirms what their horizon is and was likely their parent's as well. In those days it might have been true but today, thinking like that is just out of date - historically short-sighted."

"It is the vision of the group to which they belong. They are not accountants. They could not make a medical dead-line call. I know because I am one who decides those calls every day and anyone in my business knows that death has changed, and taxes are the subject of constant manipulation. The people who run my business strive to eliminate both. I am but one of their tools."

"My name is Brian and I'm your corporate liaison," I say to my group. The company I work for is called DL INC. and my group has come to solve the death and taxes problem. We're just getting started.

"There was much chortling around the Boardroom table when the name was suggested as the short form for "Dead Line,"" I joke. "How can a receptionist answer the phone, "Deadline Incorporated. How may I direct your call?" But "DL Incorporated," had a legal ring to it - authority in a phrase. That's what they decided to call the new creation.

In those days, the directors could not imagine an underling compressing the name further nor could they imagine the meaning the abbreviation would carry. It was a harried phone drone that actually changed the corporate direction. He answered the phone and said to the caller, "D LINC, how can I direct you?"

The people who created the technology behind the company don't answer those phones. The creators sit around tables and doodle boards and talk about what the real world is made of. The world they talk about is atomic and subatomic. Now if I asked anyone what an atom was like, if the person knew the word at all, they would likely describe an atom as a ball. And anything subatomic would be the pieces that make up the ball. They've been trained to think that way - indoctrinated some might say - brainwashed maybe.

Scientists and teachers and newscasting interpreters have used the analogy of atoms being balls because it was so easy to describe and understand. Big atoms are like big balls, small like small. Sticky spots on the outside allow atoms to attach to each other and make molecules. It gives the illusion that we, and those who know the details, really understand the fundamental structure of the world. That allows us to get on with our daily lives with some comfort. We know how things work – well somebody does. I scan my audience. "I'm going to get technical because we have a full disclosure commitment, but I've done this many times and haven't lost a single person yet," I joke.

"If atoms were like balls, the picture of a cluster would be pixelated - like a painting from a pointillist artist. Scientists at IBM made the point by moving xenon atoms to spell out the company name. The letters were clear enough, but the atoms didn't come out looking like balls in their graphic." I roll my ball bearing across the polished table to make enough noise to bring back anyone who might be dozing, then show my picture.

"The reason for the discrepancy is that atoms aren't like balls at all." I snatch up my ball with a sleight of hand that makes the bearing seem to disappear. "Each atom is like a force field – strongest at the center, decreasing to a boundary horizon. That was why the atoms in the IBM picture came out looking like Hershey Kisses. What the height represented was strength of field, not shape."

"Some curious researchers asked what was between the atoms. And that was where the ball analogy fell apart. The ball atom analogy would have you believe that between the balls there was nothing. But what is between the atoms is absolutely critical to understanding what happens at D LINC. So, I have to ask you to back up. Imagine that you never heard of atoms as balls and instead, open up to another description."

"Imagine an absolutely flat millpond. Throw a rock high in the air so it falls into the water vertically. Admire the ripples that radiate out from the impact point. Now have a friend toss in a second rock at the same time you throw in another and watch where the ripples intersect. If you look carefully, you'll find places where the ripples cancel each other and other places where the ripples combine and produce waves that are double the original height."

"Drops falling into a coffee cup can produce such patterns as well. In fact, the constructive combination of waves they make can be so energetic that a drop is thrown right up out of the coffee. The drop isn't the atom but indicates where there is so much energy that it could displace the medium. That is what an atom is like -not the ball but the energy that made it. It is an energy packet thrown up from the universal background energy sheet. If you are really curious, you can place agitators, like sticks, into calm water and create all sorts of patterns where the waves combine and interfere with each other. Each of the high points is like an atom – a point of concentrated energy the product of constructive wave interference. Try that out at the next cocktail party."

"Now between those peaks on the universal background are places of virtually undisturbed energy. That is what we deal with at DLINC. That is where we put people who want to live eternally – No death, No taxes." I'm sure I have everyone's attention.

"We get asked a lot about the 'no death' thing. Is this like the cryogenic freezing of your body? Everybody that comes to us has heard about freezing till a cure is found for whatever is about to kill them. The answer is an emphatic "NO".

"We don't save the tissue of which you are made. We save the essence – the information that allows us to rebuild you. From other atoms we create your cells and integrate them into that structure, the electrics that comprise your thoughts and feelings, the synaptic potentials that allowed you to move, maintain yourself, laugh at my jokes. We rebuild you from the information we stored. We infuse it into a body built from cell cultures and a 3D printer. Here let me show you." That's where I take the prospective clients into the animal area to meet the mice and rabbits. I open the door and usher the eight mature men and women into the next room.

"Each of these animals has died," I explain. "We have the charts and photos and DNA proof to show that the animal had no heartbeat and was brain dead. The one you are holding is now more than a decade old - post mortem." Those last words always hit home.

"It is all possible because of Quantum Computers, which have the capacity to store the colossal amount of information obtained from a whole body during the scanning process. When that detail is used to create the first stem cells, we have the template from which to grow the rest of your body cells in our culture media. We can speed things up by 3D printing large bones and organs so that you don't have to go through infancy and adolescence again. In fact, you could come out of the process with the body you had at twenty-five. That upgrading costs extra."

"Well, that's impossible," most say, and I let them dither for a while. They want to confirm the details of each animal, right down to 'Bingo', the chimpanzee at the end of the room. They are looking for the smoke and mirrors.

By the time we're through the petting zoo, most have asked how the DLINC process stores the information and that is the segue that takes us past the windows that look into the clean room. "Nobody can afford to monopolize a quantum computer just for themselves. Indeed, that is the most expensive part of the process. So as soon as the computer has acquired all the information about every atom in your body and its relation to the others, it stores the details in a safe depository. We use cubes of gold to do that."

The cubes are all lined up in the racks on the other side of the glass. There are a lot of them. The room looks to be bigger than a tennis court. "We store a person's information in a cube of gold about an inch on a side. It is inert, has all the space we need in the space between the atoms, and is easy to manipulate." I don't tell them that the Marketing Department thought it make it easier to sell also. A block of platinum didn't look nearly as exotic.

"Yes, you could have your children, or a friend take it home and put it on the mantle. We send it out in a sealed plastic box inside a decorative ceramic or wood capsule. In this container it doesn't pick up dust, is suitably protected, and quite decorative," I explain, "but you might want to take advantage of our safe storage option. Our experience is that relatives lose things like this in a move, or during housecleaning. We even had one returned from a pawnshop. Of course, if it is melted either in an accidental fire or because it was stolen, there is no way to recover the information that was stored in it. That person would be lost. It's like a Transporter malfunction in Star Trek." Everyone understands that and it usually clinches the storage contract.

"Yes, the cube costs about forty thousand dollars at current market value and after it has been purified to remove the metals that make it hard enough for jewelry. The gold we use is pure, absolutely pure. Every atom that is a contaminant has been removed."

"Yes, it isn't very much considering the total cost of the program but remember I said that the biggest cost is the use of the computer to store your information AND on the other end of the process, to restore you." There is sometimes a startled smile at that point. The process was not cremation. There was a resurrection part to the plan and that sort of chatter gets us to the end or the viewing gallery.

As I open the door to the office, someone will always comment on the single cube set aside and spotlighted. That was Marketing's idea again. I always laugh when someone asks "Why it is set aside? What makes it special?" That's when I reply as they walk into the office, "That's because it's mine."

That always brings the line of prospects to a jarring halt. I have to prompt them on to the comfortable chairs around the low, large coffee table. The energy in the room goes up a notch or three as I take my place and smile back at the circle of faces. You can tell who is already to sign the contract.

I confess that I was born before there were automobiles on the street, that I moved furniture on my bicycle to customer's homes from my dad's furniture store. I'm over a hundred years old and yet don't look a day over forty. I don't tell them that my Relink costs were covered by the company if I would be their salesperson after – and if the process worked. I was the first, and so far, only ReLink. I have a twenty-year contract, with serious penalties for welshing on my part of the bargain. But the prospective clients before me don't need to know that. Now the questions pour like a spilled pitcher.

"It's been ten years since I was ReLinked," I explain. "When I originally D-linked, I was in my eighties and had serious arthritis. I opted for the upgrade to my youth, so I didn't have the artificial hips I had when I went into the cube. I also got rid of the heart problems that were building up and avoided the dementia I was afraid I'd have to deal with. Now all those problems will return again as I age, but I know what I'm headed for and can take advantage of newer methods of addressing those issues." Incredulity was one response from his prospects; euphoria was the other. The older prospects are usually the euphoric ones. They've looked further down the tunnel they are in and see no light.

"How do you live when you Relink?" asked a puzzled client-to-be. "I thought you said there were no taxes."

"There are several ways that our accountants use to avoid paying taxes anymore. First there are gifts that a corporation can make. You have to commit all your personal wealth – and that means everything – to DL Inc. when you sign your contract. With the accumulated wealth that has been built up, we expect to soon be the largest financial organization on Earth. Your wealth earns enough to keep you in the style to which you were accustomed and to which you agreed you'd like to return." I don't tell the clients that their money earns us a lot more than it earns them. "The proceeds of your investment can be paid to you in monthly instalments as a gift from DL Inc. without tax." Several nod.

"But we were going to make large gifts to our grandchildren when we died."

"But when you thought of that, you didn't know you were going to live, did you?" I counter. The questioner nodded in agreement. "Any gifts you make after this presentation and in the past five years will affect the contract, we can offer you. By reducing the investment, you are making in your future," I emphasize the pronoun, "you change the earliest date on which you can ReLink or the age to which you can be ReLinked." The personal interest angle always works with these people.

"DL Inc also has built a variety of accommodations around the world, where you can live, free, providing you wait long enough to Relink. That is covered under a part of the laws governing perpetual care. You may be familiar with that charge made at the time of interment with previous relatives. It takes on new meaning here. We are obliged, as a corporation, to provide you with perpetual food and lodging and are supervised to see that we have set aside adequate funds to do that."

"How long does it take to Relink?" one person asked.

"One hundred and eighty days is required so you should think about the time of year you want to experience when you ReLink." I usually go on to describe the virtues of each season. "Always assume the sale," my mentors had taught me.

"So, when we come back," the older man with the grandchildren asked, "we could be younger looking than our grandchildren? Would we think like kids again?"

"That is not beyond possibility, but it would be your choice to do so. You might decide you'd like to be young again." Both seniors shook their heads but smiled broadly. The woman added what she'd heard to her notebook.

"You would still find you had the wisdom of your current age though and could choose how you'd use the new energy of your second adulthood." The smiles got even broader and there was a leg bump as well. "They'll buy the premium package, I'll bet."

One woman who had not asked any questions until then spoke up. "What does it feel like to DeLink?" she asked, and everyone leaned forward a bit as I considered my answer.

"I was nervous on the day I came in," I say. "But I'd said my 'Au revoirs.'" I like that word instead of 'Good-byes', "to all my friends and hoped I'd see them again. A few have put their ReLinking day further ahead than mine but I'm expecting to meet up with them someday. You have to get out of your clothes and lie down on a warm padded cot rather like a tanning bed or beach and you close your eyes. You hear a humming sound and then nothing. It's not painful, just dark. Well, that's what I recalled when I woke up. It was like being asleep. When I came back, I was covered by a nice warm sheet, and I felt so refreshed. The light was soft, my favourite music was quietly playing in the background. I looked over and found some clothes on the chair beside the bed. Somebody came in and asked how I was …"

"So, you don't recall being in Heaven or Hell?"

"Nope. Don't recall anything at all. I just woke up and found I didn't ache; the air was cool, and I felt great! It was just like I'd gone to sleep and woken up except it was ten years later, but I had the body of someone fifty years younger. Maybe that is what Heaven is except you have to learn to play the harp there." There were chuckles around the circle. They always like that line.

"I walked out of my room into the hall," I continue, "and a nice young man met me and took me to an office where I got my updated Driver's License, and Debit Cards. All purchases are on Debit Cards that subtract the item from your generous monthly allowance. I've never had a problem. They say I don't need a Health Card, but you get one anyway. It's easier than explaining to Officials that you don't get sick. And there is still the risk of accidents. They gave me a hundred dollars in starting money and the fob to a new electric car. You have to pay for that ahead as part of your package, if you want it. The GPS in the car took me to my apartment downtown in one of DL Inc.'s buildings. It was all furnished as I'd arranged. A salad lunch was in the refrigerator with instructions to the nearest grocery store. I found my own way to the Beer Store." More chuckles rippled around the group. "Is that enough?"

"Sounds like he died and went to heaven," quipped one listener to his partner.

"Could I use the details in the cube to make a clone of myself?" asked one of the single men. I always like to hear that change in the pronoun. This isn't abstract anymore. That person is a certain sale.

"Nobody has asked for that, but the simple answer is, 'Yes'. It would be treated like partners – husband and wife or whatever. We would have to change your identification by inserting the initial 'A' into your name. Your clone brother would be identified as 'B'. There would be the same costs associated with the ReLinking that would have to be paid for ahead of time. You might think of that for a subsequent DeLinking. During your new life, you might seek to earn enough to finance such a companion as well as your own repeat procedure."

One aged prospect who walked with a walker asked with a croaky voice, "What do you do in your new life? At what could you work?"

"If you are planning to ReLink in more than twenty years or if you purchase the 'Youth Package', we already include in your contract a retraining program that will occur over your first year. If you chose not to retrain, you can live as your contract has guaranteed, in one of DL Inc, accommodations. You need not be gainfully employed but the retraining program cost is not refundable."

"What were you in your first life?" asked a matron who had arrived without a partner.

"I was many things. As a teen, I helped my dad install gas lighting in homes nearby. When electricity became available, I sold light bulbs and furniture as I said. I delivered chairs and tables on my bicycle. Later I worked at selling the first radios. They had tubes and needed an antenna to receive distant stations. I was young and agile enough to climb poles or trees to string the antennae. Then I worked in selling stocks and bonds. When I ReLinked, I came to work for the company. I like what I do here now because I can meet so many interesting people who are tired of wrestling with what they always thought were life's certainties. It is very rewarding to help so many, I find."

"If we chose to ReLink in fifty years nobody on staff now would be around to carry out the process. What procedures are in place to guarantee we will be ReLinked as we plan?"

"Well just to be clear, I will probably be here, though I won't be running the Relink programs. Many of our technicians will likely be relinked so you shouldn't count us out. You'll likely see familiar faces – sort of like at the resort you might have gone back to year after year. But whether or not the same people are on staff or not, your relink will be accomplished by computers."

"All our procedures are computer operated now. They automatically update and protect themselves with encrypted software using our Quantum Computers. The entire facility is powered by geothermal-electric power that will run for millennia. Heat from deep in the earth is converted directly into electricity by an array of exchangers at a depth of ten thousand meters. There is no steam intermediary. We sell energy to the grid, but it only goes one way to a maximum level that leaves abundant power for internal needs. We make any spare parts we need from the same 3D processes we use to make bones and teeth. The system is in a constant state of self-monitoring and self-repair."

"I can see you've run out of questions," I was about to say when a hand went up from grandmother. "What happens to … you know … our body? Do the kids have a funeral?"

"We can arrange for them to have a service in our facility," I say. I don't remind them that they won't have a pot to piss in because they will have signed over every last nickel to DL Inc. "The body will be reverently respected and will be composted in our cemetery. There is no need for an urn or headstone because you won't be dead, will you?" That takes a moment to think through. "Now I know more questions will occur to you," I continue as I address the group. "We want to answer them all. So as part of your presentation, we offer you a three-day, free, all-expenses-paid experience of what your new life will be like by staying here with us. This is one of our accommodations and has all the programs and amenities you can expect if you sign up. We can't make this offer to you again, - that is why we want to be sure to answer all your questions. So, if you'll follow me to the Concierge, I'll see you all checked in."

2

George and Mabel Twilling found their luggage already in their room. They liked their large rolling cases that they didn't have to lift onto the bed to unload. Their years of vacation cruising coupled with growing back problems had confirmed that lifting luggage was not in their future. They opted for the old steamer trunk style in which you hung garments on one side and set shirts, underwear, shoes and medical needs in tip-up shelves on the other. In the up position, the set of shelves pressed against the one above to keep their clothes in place and nice and flat, so they didn't need re-ironing. It didn't matter that the luggage was big enough to carry an adult. There were lots of young people about to lift luggage for them – taxi drivers, porters and the like. Excess baggage on airlines was not a problem. They could afford first class and all that went with it.

In fact, it was thinking of the loss of such privilege that made Mabel cringe. To cover the fear, she pushed a chair in front of the open luggage to unload it comfortably. Her hand brushed the pure silk blouse and cashmere sweater with pride as she lifted them into the shelving in the closet beside her high-fashion evening wear. They'd come first class but if they took up the offer, they'd leave with an allowance – 'well maybe a hundred years from now and with the made-over body that she had so enjoyed flaunting, and a pension to get by on,' she admitted to herself. She'd be expected to give up everything even liquidate the jewels that were her grandmother's.

On the other hand, what else would happen to the gems. She and George had decided to have no children - they got in the way of the lifestyle they imagined for themselves. Her own brother's children hadn't crossed their threshold in so long, she wouldn't recognize them if they did. She had not thought to will them to children she didn't know. Too late anyway according to that pitchman. He suggested that from the time they walked in the door all their assets were frozen and had to be surrendered if they took up the offer to Delink.

"I wonder if we'd get our old clothes back?" she asked George who was wheezing from a chair by the window. He'd left all his clothes in his case. He didn't need to unload them. They were just more of what he had on now. He'd only opened his trunk for a few puffs of is oxygen tank.

"Well, I expect it would cost extra and by then, would you want to wear clothes that were so out of fashion. I doubt they'd fit your new body anyway."

"How about our suitcases?"

"Same thing I expect. In the future, you probably walk to the mirror and ask for a set of clothes and something makes them like a 3D printer. It scans you and three minutes later they drop into the tray below. But that isn't what you wanted to know was it. You were wondering what happens to the diamonds and gold coins you sewed into the lining of your trunk for an emergency."

For someone so old and addled most of the time, he sure has a mind for money, Mabel thought. "I think I'll go for a walk around, she declared. "Want to come?"

"I'm going to have a nap," George said as he lay down on the nearest of the twin beds to the window. He didn't take off his shoes. So, what if he left dirt on the bedspread. They were paying for the room. That's what washing machines and staff were for. And besides he couldn't bend over to take them off or put them on later anyway.

"I'll give you your meds now and be back to get you for dinner," Mabel said when she saw him sag onto the bed. She took pills from a bottle in her purse and brought a crystal tumbler of water from the washroom. "Here," she said holding them out to him.

George rolled himself up on one elbow with difficulty, tossed the pills down and chased them with the water before handing the glass back and rolling down again. He didn't notice Mabel fluff her hair in the mirror, check her makeup and give a fresh touch of cologne to the picture she presented.

As the door clicked shut, George shut his eyes against the light from the window and sighed carefully. *Who was it that said growing old was not for sissies?* he thought. He never knew anyone could ache as he did. Well, he was all for calling it quits any time. Yesterday would have been fine. He remembered playing tennis and the strength he enjoyed in his youth. He took it for granted then. Not now! He wondered if there were any more papers to sign and get this job done. He'd asked twice if everything was done when Mabel went to the washroom after the pitch Instead of waking up in a couple hours back in this painful prison he was in, there was the hope of waking up a new man. With a smile on his face, he drifted off into a thick sleep.

Mabel waited for an elevator at the end of the hallway. Again, she checked her makeup and silhouette in the mirror behind the flowers on the table. The surgery had done its job and she showed it. The elevator pinged and she turned with a swirl that was designed to spread a cloud of her expensive perfume about her as she stepped into the car. The young man returning from a room service delivery, ran his eyes over her as he asked which floor.

"Main Lobby," she replied with a smile.

Mabel was twenty-five years younger than George. She was the trophy wife and knew it. She was the confirmation of the virility belying the over-the-hill state of her husband. He had a fortune stashed away after half a lifetime in successful stock market trading that happened after he divorced his first wife. She'd spotted his star on the rise, made her play and both became what the other wanted. But this expedition to DL Inc was not something she saw coming.

George's health was declining steeply lately – the ravages of high blood pressure. He really wanted the reincarnation that this place promised. Frankly she'd missed it with all her preoccupation on own face lifting and body sculpting procedures. Maybe it was because he saw what was happing to her that he decided to go for the bigger package, so to speak. She was sceptical. If it's too good to be true… and all that. The part that made her scared was the threat of liquidation of all their assets. She wanted to check that out with the company rep. Suppose she didn't want to be born again. Like why would she need that? She already had it!

"Brian," she called as soon as she spotted him in the lobby. He beamed a smile back when he spotted her. "Could we talk a moment?"

Brian steered her to a corner chair from which they could watch people pass. She brushed against Brian as she passed, aware of the attention she had aroused in him. She explained where George was and that she was out for a walk. "I wanted to ask about what happens if I don't want to go through with the process. It makes me nervous thinking about it."

"You are right to be so," Brian placated. "That shows the analytical skills that brought you here in the first place. Because most couples hold their assets jointly, both have to agree to surrender all those assets in order for the process to happen. Of course, that occurs at the time of Delink-ing. However, you can choose to Relink at different times."

It was as she thought. Everything goes. All George's assets were in his name. She only got them if she inherited them.

"Is there a minimum time you must be Delinked?" she asked past a frown.

"The time we have set as the shortest Relinking is four years – two for legal to wrap up its business and a little less than two for building the new body you will inhabit. Most technicalities are wrapped up in a matter of weeks but Legal wants to leave lots of time to do things right. But immediately Relinking in such a short time would be a rather expensive way to do a divorce, if that is what you're thinking. It is rather like setting up an expensive company and collapsing it immediately. Not sound business." He looked at her carefully.

"You could simply walk away here and now. The consequences are that we couldn't offer this opportunity to you again and of course the assets pass into DL Inc's control as soon as George underwent his procedure." Mabel jumped at the fact he seemed to know she was not a joint partner in George's wealth. "But you are letting your anxiety run away with you here. Both of you can step confidently from a life of declining ability to be reborn into the life you've always wanted." Mabel's lips were tight.

"I can see you've looked after yourself well," Brian observed boldly, "and you have accomplished what few others could in preserving the stunning person you are, but your striking appearance is as good as current skill can accomplish."

Mabel felt flushed, as though he was looking through her clothes. She had always enjoyed the looks of men, actually cultured the attention with her discrete flirting, but in those cases, she was firmly in control. This was a little too close to the bone, as it were, and she definitely was not in control at the moment.

"You could have that and more through De and Relinking and have years more of happy life as well. George's current condition, and the condition of many others," he waved at those in the lobby, "are a testament to what awaits us all in the near future if you decide to go home … alone."

The searing analysis was enough to make Mabel pull back into the chair then quickly rise to her feet. "Well thank you, Brian. It is another of the many facts we need to reflect on," she blurted. "See you around," she continued around a brittle smile and made a hasty retreat towards the Lounge.

"A glass of white wine," she ordered to the person polishing glasses as she swept past the bar heading for the wide windows that overlooked the frozen lake and vista beyond. She dropped into a smooth black leather chair with wide arms and shoulder-high back. "Good support', she assessed as she wiggled to get comfortable. Her wine appeared before she had settled, "Can I get you anything to go with it?" asked the smiling lady in the starched black and white uniform.

"No," Mabel replied tersely. She took a deep gulp and looked out at the sun shining on the ice and granite cliffs beyond, multicoloured in the sunshine. The scraggly trees clung like torn black cobwebs across the frosted stones. Such vistas had always stimulated creative thought in her. She needed that now.

In moments she could feel her frustration sliding away and her initial resolve returning. She had what all these others were looking for – youth back again. The problem was that she wanted youth and security – financial independence. She wanted to never have to ask the price of anything again. De and Relinking was going to give her the chance to start all over in exchange for the financial independence she already would have if she inherited George's wealth. There was no guarantee that she'd find anyone well enough endowed, financially of course, to keep her in the manner she expected in the future. With each sip, that alternative blurred a bit.

By the time she'd reached the bottom of her glass, the problem had been resolved in her mind. Well, it wasn't as though she hadn't been thinking of this solution for quite a while. It would be convenient if George would die before he Delinked. That would leave her a wealthy widow and she could thumb her nose at the place as she walked out the door. She didn't have to wait a century. There would be no wondering about her financial security. Both were here now!

"Are you one of the staff?" asked the soft voice at her elbow. Mabel swiveled to see the lady with the notebook that had been in their presentation group.

"No," Mabel said. "I was in the same group presentation as you. I remember you taking notes."

"I'm sorry," the senior said, somewhat flustered. "You look so young. I thought you might work here."

Mabel stifled a small shiver of delight and sucked in a bigger breath. "Come and join me," she invited, summoning her better behaviour from her social closet. The lady placed careful hands on each arm of the chair and lowered herself slowly to a perch on the edge of the seat. The waitron was behind her immediately offering a pillow to fill the space behind the senior. "Is that more comfortable?"

"Yes thank-you," the lady smiled sideways. The server immediately caught the cue that her guest had a back or neck problem and couldn't twist so she stepped around so the grandmother could see her directly – and probably hear her as well.

"Would you like something to drink?" she asked.

"Could you get me some cool water, with no ice and squeeze a wedge of lemon into it? I can't do it with these old hands anymore." She wiggled her swollen arthritic knuckles.

The server responded with a radiant smile. "Of course," she beamed. "And you Madame?" she asked looking at Mabel.

"The same … please," remembering the addition in the nick of time. Older people took the use of such civilities as the badge of upbringing. The waitress swept up Mabel's empty wineglass and backed away.

"I thought you looked familiar," the lady said evasively as the server stepped away. "It makes me embarrassed when I don't remember people."

"It is one of the aspects of their presentation I would recommend they attend to," Mabel said. "They didn't introduce us." Her voice was clipped. She had to quickly change mental gears back to civility. "The least they could have done was give us those sticky name tags to wear. My name is Mabel," she finished and stuck out her hand.

"I'm Emma Werner, and I'm sorry but we can't shake hands. Mine are so sore. My grandchildren showed me how to fist bump gently. Would that be OK?"

Mabel laughed and they did.

The server returned with her silver tray. Two stemmed glasses of water, ever so gently misted by the beverage inside, stood at attention on a linen disc that protected the tray. She set crocheted doilies on the glass tabletop in front of the women and the glasses on them.

"I haven't seen crocheted doilies since I left our home to move into the Retirement Home," Emma said in admiration.

"I make them myself," the server said with pride. "My Grandmother taught me." Mabel thought she caught the faintest hint of an Irish brogue in the waitress's voice. "The management says that the guests appreciate them."

"Let me remember to tell them they are right," Emma said. She made to reach for her glass. The waitress saw it might be out of reach and moved the glass and coaster slightly closer. "Thank-you," Emma said acknowledging the kindness. She lifted her glass with both hands and took a careful sip.

Mabel, watching the cameo from the side, thought, *I have wondered who made those things. I thought machines did it.* She raised her glass smoothly in a toast with Emma.

"I wonder if it will look the same when I see it next?" Emma asked waving out the window. "Do you think it has changed much since the first explorers stood here?"

"I can't say I've ever thought of that," Mabel replied.

"Günter and I were farmers and the children of farmers. We are so used to looking at the land we have taken care of, I can't ever remember not doing so." She sat so still looking into the distance that Mabel wondered what she should say. She had never thought about 'looking after' dirt. *That's really what land was. Dirt with location. Who looked after it? How could you look after dirt? It is yet another example of how addled old people got,* she mused.

Emma had gotten into a mental rut it seemed. She was reciting her youth on the farm, growing things, bushels per acre, first and second cuts, selling part of your crop ahead to be sure the mortgage was covered. *As incomprehensible as Chinese*, thought Mabel.

"Have you set your Time?" Mabel asked.

"The children and grandchildren are coming up for goodbyes on the weekend. We'll do it on Sunday at church time. It seems appropriate somehow."

"Didn't your children object to not being left an inheritance?"

"We raised our kids to be self-sufficient. Hanna married a businessman in town. They have their first child – Elizabeth. She's a toddler. Hans and Ernst are engineers. They make me so proud!" She drifted into a short reverie then realized she'd stopped talking and jumped back in before Mabel could say anything. "They're each making more money than the farm brought in on a good year. Every one of them knew how much work farming was. Every one of them said 'no thanks'. When we sold the farm, we'd thought to make a big donation to the Church, but our congregation got combined with the congregations in Larkwell and Benton Center. They said it would make the new congregation self-supporting. Do you think they knew the history there? Not likely!" She was puffed out with righteous indignation.

"We weren't sending that sort of money to People Like That," she declared with extreme diction, "and certainly not to some bureaucracy off in the city. So, we decided we'd take up this offer and relink in 2070. We want to go back to the land we grew up on. It's in the Green Belt so it can't be sold for housing. The company who bought the property wanted it to spread the manure from their chicken operation and then grow grain for the new barn full of birds. Heaven's, they have thousands of birds." She drifted off in thought again.

"We could be labourers again; save enough to buy a farm and do it all over again. We'd be able to look after our Grandchildren that way. Wouldn't that be twist? I think there is a religion that says if you live a poor life, you come back to get another chance to fix your mistakes. I wonder if we'll remember the blunders we made?" She smiled again at the thought.

"I thought that was a guarantee. You'd have all the wisdom of this life to apply to the next."

"Hmmmm," Emma said and took another sip at her glass.

"It will be dinner soon. I have to go and get George up from his nap," Mabel said assertively to end the conversation. She set her water on the tabletop. She did not notice the reflexive twitch of Emma's hand to put it on the doily. Emma stared at the film of water that spread from the base on the glass out to make a mark where none had been. Mabel was gone before Emma pursed her lips and shook her head.

The conversation had had a dozy quality to it that Mabel managed to dispel to the rhythm of her clipped steps across the lobby floor. Her thinking was re-engaging the plan that was in mid formation before she was interrupted by Emma what's-her-name. The descending numbers on the elevator display helped. George took two sleeping pills every night. It was the maximum allowable with his blood pressure, cholesterol meds, inhalers and other pain medication. It would be easy to add one or two more to the mix. He just chugged the cup containing them back without counting them. There wouldn't be so much that he'd be sick and throw it all up - just enough to see him to sleep and keep him there. The elevator doors slid open. A couple pulling oxygen bottles on carts stepped out mumbling incomprehensibly to each other through the masks that covered their mouths and noses.

As the rising elevator called out each passing floor, Mabel found herself mentally reviewing and confirming the pill count in the bed-time meds cup. Mentally running over the pill bottles on the counter in the washroom where she'd aligned them, distracted her so that she was surprised when she suddenly found herself in front of their room door. Her keycard, on the lanyard doubled and tried stylishly to her belt opened the door with a clack. George was already up and setting down the telephone.

"I wondered if you got lost," he asked. "Isn't it dinner in about half an hour?"

Mabel was surprised to find him up. He looked so stupid standing there in his saggy briefs and undershirt, hair all askew with an already forgotten phone in his hand. "Of Course," she snapped. "I'm not the one who's usually late." She slid back the closet door to survey what she'd brought to wear to dinner. "Put the phone back," she ordered.

"Oh," he responded looking at his hand somewhat surprised to see it still held the receiver. He set it back. George had not moved his clothes from his case. It stood open at the end of his bed. He took out the hanger that held his pressed suit pants securely. The belt was already through the loops. He pulled them on then the shirt from the next hanger in line. He remembered to tug it down straight, so the buttons lined up with the holes. He started buttoning from the bottom ones he could see.

As he worked his way up his shirt, he glanced at his wife standing in her skimpy underwear across the room, slipping the selected dress from its hanger. *More engineering in that stuff than the CN tower*, he thought.

"Leave the top two open," Mabel directed from across the room where she was arranging her black dinner dress with the dramatic neckline.

"I know," George replied with irritation. He stopped doing up buttons when he couldn't see them as he tried to look down his front. The exercise left him wheezing. He slid down into his chair and took a few breaths from his portable tank, still parked in the bottom of his case, then added two puffs from the inhaler beside it.

"Socks, then shoes," Mabel called from the bathroom where she was freshening her makeup.

One more day of that God damned woman's carping, George thought. *Just because I forgot one time.* He slid a pair of black socks from his case drawer and struggled into them. *Just one more day*, he thought. With slip-on shoes on his feet, he stood and pulled on the suit coat that stared at him from the case then sat down again to calm his breathing. He was ready.

A toilet flush and running water presaged Mabel's breezy arrival back into the room to select jewellery. George watched her dither from the other side of the room. A black onyx inverted teardrop pendant drew attention to the skin it lay on and the cleavage below. As she put on the matching earrings, she eyed George across the room using the mirror. "Put your room key – the thing on the string - around your neck. It's how they track your meals, and movement around the building."

George couldn't figure out what the thing on a string meant. He simply sat there. In exasperation, Mabel came across, picked it up from the bedside table and flipped the lanyard over his head so the identity lay across his chest. He looked down at the plaque resting on his thousand-dollar suit. *God that looks stupid*, he thought then realized he was missing something.

The missing thing made him anxious, and his breathing started to speed up. It came to him – 'my pen. I'm missing my pen.' He didn't see his pen anywhere but there was one on the writing table on the other side of his chair. He picked it up and made to slip it into his inside jacket pocket. It wouldn't go. He folded back his lapel and tried again and again to put the pen where he had carried it his whole working life. He gave up and stabbed it into his shirt pocket, but the pen left a blue mark on his white shirt. He gritted his teeth, closed his lapel, and looked up blandly. Mabel was selecting a perfume from the bottles ranked before her. George closed his eyes and concentrated on slowing his breathing.

"Are you ready then?" Mabel said at last. She brought his long-lasting inhaler to him in a cloud of expensive chemistry. "Take this before we go – just to be sure."

George did as he was told. Buoyed by the shot of steroids and the increasing distance from the cause of his breathlessness, he followed her out of the room to the elevator. She had the car waiting. It was a short trip down.

3

At dinner, another couple and an Information Officer sat at their table. DL Inc had found that it was just plain efficient to have a member of their staff with each client during the run up to their event to keep things moving in the right direction and to immediately dispel misinformation or address last-minute jitters or questions.

"Your rooms are comfortable?" Monique asked, laying her burgundy leather folder in the empty place at the table.

Everyone mumbled agreement.

Their server appeared and announced what was being served based on the preferences and restrictions dictated in their applications. Mabel had carte blanche, but constraints dictated the amounts and kind of food for each of the others. George was surprised when he was told that there was an excellent non-alcoholic wine-like product that had just become available and was approved for the mix of medications he was taking. He agreed to try some. It was served with all the flourish of any exotic wine and George was surprised at how delicious he found it. Mabel ordered a dry martini.

"I could get used to this," George said as the server refilled his glass. With the reading of the label, the testing of the beverage by both of them, Mabel and George were able to ignore the business that was obviously going on with the other couple. Some papers were signed and then put into the leather folder. George was savouring his new beverage when Monique concluded her duties and looked at her communicator, pointed it at his badge, and looked at what came up. She nodded and smiled across at him. Her actions said all his paperwork was complete. Mabel missed the exchange in her examination of the label and origin of his beverage and the arrival of her second martini.

"We came up yesterday," explained their tablemates when Monique had excused herself, business complete. "We just signed for our Delinking appointment tomorrow after lunch. It was the one document we didn't sign when we came in."

"Yes. You can't proceed till you signed your life away," they both laughed at the joke. "And even then, you can always back our right up till the last minute, but you know what that means. No, we're happy to be moving on. Saw our last sunset for a while and this will be our last supper for a long time. Sounds Biblical doesn't it." They both laughed.

"Except we're planning to celebrate," continued the one with the bandages from his recent surgery. "I wonder if that stuff you have is on our list?" the man asked looking at George's drink.

The meal took on a party atmosphere for the others - not Mabel. She smiled at all the right places and made small talk to fill a book. The food was extraordinary – small portions but so flavourful that you really didn't need much to make you feel satisfied. But all she really wanted to do was get out of there. Could they just finish and go to their rooms? She'd see George had his meds, she could pack, and tomorrow after the formalities were done, she could ship George back home by FedEx or whatever and be back in their penthouse by this time tomorrow. The meal finally ended with the help of another martini.

As they rode the last floors alone, Mabel interrupted the silence. "I'm not signing that paper, George. I'm not going to do this!" The car jerked to a stop as though it had heard her. But the door opened, and it was just their floor. George just sighed. He needed his meds and another jolt from the oxygen bottle.

When he was able to breathe again, he asked if she'd like a brandy before bed. He was going to have the last glass in the bottle he'd had at dinner. He'd brought it back from the table with him.

Room service brought it on a silver tray. A handsome blown glass balloon on a short stem stood beside a handsome bottle of Martell XO cognac. The bottle itself looked like an enlargement of one of Mabel's perfume bottles, a tribute to an artist's skill and Marketing's imagination. The non-stemmed empty glass for his beverage stood like an embarrassment on the other side of the tray. It seemed to be trying to escape.

George rescued the utilitarian tumbler and poured the last of his bottle into it. There were only a few swallows left. "I'll pour yours?" he called through the open door of the bathroom where she was drying off from her shower. She came through in one of those thick terrycloth robes the hotel provided.

George was looking out the window as the moon rose over the lake. "I just put in a splash," George explained. "I didn't know if you'd like it."

"Here's your meds," she said thrusting an eggcup of coloured pills into his hand as she swirled past.

Mabel stared at the dribble he'd poured into her snifter. "You can't send it back," she admonished as she held the bowl to warm the glass and then took a smell and sip that finished the sample in one glug. "Yep! That's good stuff." She poured a generous refill.

George stared into coloured collection and was about to chug them all. "I've finished my wine. I need some water," he said.

Mabel gave a theatrical sigh, set down her drink and stomped as loudly as the soft carpeting allowed, across the room. George struggled out of the soft chair to go to bed. "Could you make the water cool?" George called out.

The sound of mutterings and a dumped tumbler of water followed by a lengthy running of the tap finally stopped and Mabel returned. She snapped the glass down on the bedside table towards which George was headed. George silently chugged the collection in his hand and chased them with the water that was ice cold.

Mabel was working on her tumbler of cognac and staring out the black window when he turned out his bedside light.

He woke immediately at the tap on the door two hours later. "Coming", he called then took a puff on his ventilator and pulled a dressing gown from his trunk.

"She's ready," he said to the attendant in the hall. Two women came in and gently lifted Mabel from the chair where she'd fallen asleep, onto the gurney. "She really didn't want to walk down there. I explained that to Brian."

"Yes, we got that message."

"So, she just took a couple sleeping pills. Brian said that was not a problem."

"Would you like us to come and get you at eight?" one attendant asked.

"No, I can make it on my own I think."

When they left, George knew he wouldn't sleep. He hadn't taken his sleeping pills and he wanted to watch the last sunrise he'd see for more than a century. So, he'd just stay up and look at the night beyond the glass. When he next saw the sun come up, they said he'd be a young man and his recently departed wife would be an eighty-year-old hag – unless she'd found someone else to fund another cycle. Not his problem. In fact, it sounded like Heaven.

4

Mabel felt herself drifting out of sleep towards wakefulness but not enough to open her eyes. What she saw through closed eyelids was darkness. It surprised her that she was sleeping on her back. She usually slept on her left side. The effort to roll over was too much. She felt herself slide pleasantly back into sleep.

When next she surfed the wave that lifted her to wakefulness, she felt so rested and renewed. She still left her eyes closed, revelling in the sense of release and renewal. *Haven't slept like that for years*, she thought. She was aware that she was naked under the sheet that covered her. The memory of other naked nights brought a chuckle. *Guess I just dropped my robe on the floor after my drink*, she mused.

She remembered she hadn't closed the curtains. That sun would be dazzlingly bright. Best just to roll away from the windows to avoid a sunbeam in the eye. Still with eyes closed, she listened for the sound of George's breathing. Nothing. She held her own breath and listened intently. She could not hear a sound from her husband. There were some distant institutional sounds. *That's the elevator*, she thought. *That sounds like a room-service cart rattling by*. There was not a sound from the bed behind her. *Well, I guess the medicine did its job*, she thought. This was her first day of widowhood. A line of music from a Lehar musical floated through her mind. *I wonder what a grieving and obscenely wealthy widow wears, besides an ear-to-ear smile*, was her next thought. She interrupted the inventory of her wardrobe in the closet. *Wonder what time it is?*

She opened one eye, the one raised above the pillow not buried in it. *Hmmmph,* she sniffed. *Where did the clock go? Did I knock it off the bedside table?* she wondered. She closed her eyes again reviewing the image from going to bed the night before. Yes, there was a digital clock and a shaded lamp over it – twist-button switch on the base. She opened her eyes again. No clock. No lamp. Only a white wall. She closed her eyes again. Wasn't she still at the hotel? She rolled back and looked over to George's bed. – another white wall.

"What the hell…" She struggled to sit up. Four white walls and a door. No window, no bathrobe lying beside the bed. White light panels in the white ceiling. A white freeform chair was on the wall at the foot of the bed. It looked like black slacks and her favourite coloured long-sleeved top were draped over the back, underwear on the seat, black walking shoes beneath. "I didn't pack that stuff," she muttered.

As she moved to throw back the heavy sheet over her, a tug came at her wrist as it brushed a deep fold. She was wearing a white plastic bracelet, two fingers wide. *What's that. I'd never buy anything that ugly*, she thought, then she squinted at the black block printing. 'Mabel Twinning,' it read. What stopped her breath were the numbers after the name. '2070/6/1'.

5

"What kind of a joke is this?" She was getting annoyed now. But the shock of a quick look at her torso where the faint scars from her cosmetic surgeries should be, showed they were somehow missing. She didn't even move to pull up the sheet when the door slid open and what looked like a nurse greeted her. "Good morning, Mabel."

"You bastard," Mabel screamed at the smiling face sliding the door closed as she stepped into the room. "You God-forsaken Rotten, Son of a Bitch. Ahhhhh." Mabel hurled the only thing at hand – her pillow - at the startled woman. The attendant hurried towards Mabel pulling a can of medicated spray from her pants pocket as she came. A spray in Mabel's face had the calming effect the nurse wanted. Mabel fell back on the bed like a puppet whose strings had been cut but she didn't stop swearing. The nurse just grabbed Mabel's wrists and held her, so she didn't damage something.

"We've gone to a lot of trouble to get bring you here today. We don't want you to hurt yourself. There," she said as Mabel finally ran out of all the epithets she knew and the effort to screech them again.

"Most people suffer a Relinking confusion, but I've never seen anyone so distressed. It is temporary, I assure you." She watched Mabel start to relax so released her restraint on her patient's wrists. "I can see you're feeling calmer already." Mabel tried to clench her fist and pound it on the bed, but the fist was loose, and the arm fell limply.

"What I came to tell you is that breakfast is ready in the cafeteria," The nurse bent to pick up the pillow and tuck it behind Mabel's head. "You need to get dressed. I'm here to help if you need it and then we offer limousine service." She nodded to the wheelchair. "On your first days, you'll want some help until the physio catches up. As soon as you're dressed, we can get the day started," she said brightly.

Her rage, and the spray medication left Mabel feeling enervated. She simply lay back staring at the ceiling cursing in every way she knew. Eventually the nurse had pushed and pulled her into her clothes and run a comb through Mabel's stylishly short hair. Mabel fell into a doze as the nurse wheeled her to the dining room.

Mabel awoke in an alcove of the dining area. There were four other tables, none occupied. All were white topped but had no chairs at any of them. A breakfast of what looked like yogurt over some sort of fruit salad, a toasted croissant waiting for jam or butter at the side and a pale amber steaming beverage that was probably tea. Yes, she smelled it now. It was Earl Grey.

Hunger took over when interest failed. She shovelled the bowl clean. Chomped down the bun and slurped her way to the bottom of the tea. She was embarrassed to finally stop and look down the front of what had been a favourite top and find it covered in crumbs and a streak of yogurt. She was glad her back was to the other tables.

Without even being asked, the nurse returned with an elegant shawl in hand to wrap around her shoulders. *It's a soft wool, probably cashmere*, Mabel thought though she couldn't find a label that said so. She was finding the room cool – and it conveniently covered the yogurt mess.

"Everyone finds it takes a while to get their body temperature regulation working. And that shawl looks wonderful on you." The flattering words felt as good as the shawl. "So, from here, we go to the gym. Your trainer is waiting," the attendant said when she saw the cleaned dishes.

"I really want to go back to my room," Mabel said over her shoulder to the nurse. She said it as a directive, and it was met with a walking silence.

"You'll feel better after the gym."

They turned from the white hallway with the black floor through a doorway that opened on the right. The room was about the size of a tennis court, mirrored all round to head height and a-tangle with white painted metalwork and reflections on chromed steel. Her attendant stopped in front of the first machine – a treadmill. Somehow the design hadn't changed much in fifty years. It still was a wide belt on which to walk, handles to hold and a control panel. Mabel faced the inevitable, hoisted herself from the wheelchair and stepped up onto the belt. One slow step, two, three with a hand on each side rail got her to the blank console.

"Is this thing ..." she called over her shoulder.

"Good morning, Mabel," came a new voice. It took her a look-around to realize it came from the machine. Her attendant with the wheelchair had already disappeared.

"You're going to warm up slowly," said the machine. "The belt will start in three seconds," and then it counted down. The belt hummed into action and Mabel stepped forward. Three steps more and she felt she would fall. "Bigger steps," called the machine. "Step out a bit more." Music started softly from somewhere in the machine.

That's my favourite track from ... before, she thought. It helped. She got into stride with the music. A few minutes later, at the end of the first selection in the mix, the machine suggested cordially, "You could probably take off your shawl now. Do you want me to stop while you do?"

Mabel realized she was warm and starting to perspire. Without breaking stride, she flipped it over the arm of the treadmill. It gave her a momentary thrill to see herself in the mirror, flick off the item with such casual savoire-faire. She also noted her new silhouette in the reflection. *Nice*, she thought. The pace picked up just a bit just as the music did. In ten minutes, she was stepping at a rate of two steps a second. The console said so and the music track was coming to an end.

"It is time for a rehydration break and a bathroom break," the machine suggested abruptly. "I'm going to slow down starting in three, two, one." The machine coasted easily to rest. The hall door opened to her right and a canister on wheels rolled in by itself. "An electrolyte and protein supplement," explained the machine. "The toilets are on the right. Can you walk, unassisted?"

Mabel realized she had turned and stepped down from the treadmill with close to her old casualness. "I'm OK, I think," she replied. She sipped the foamy drink in the plastic cup that rose out of the canister on a rising tray. *Chocolate*, she thought. "It can't be wrong if it starts with chocolate," she said aloud to the treadmill.

"I'm glad you approve," the treadmill replied. "Your workout will continue in ten minutes."

When Mabel stepped onto the track after her washroom break, she was still mulling over the instructions on the wall beside the paperless toilet facility. Only after she had started walking again did she realize there were two other people in the room — each moving slowly on different treadmills. One was a very buff looking male, the other an attractive woman. She had no time to assess further; her treadmill was talking to her and raising the pace.

Mabel lost track of the number of short work-out sessions that filled the morning. They gradually became more intricate and demanding and were all under the direction of Cameron, "your personal trainer," said the treadmill when he handed her off for weight training. Cameron was a taller version of the drinkbot — more like a post that held up something massive. He had a voice like those she remembered from the gym long ago. He said things like "feel the burn" and "fire up those abs", and "three more reps". He congratulated her after every set. He corrected every stance using the mannequin on the video screen in his chest and told her why. By the time another of those drinks from her short companion would not fill the void, Cameron told her it was lunchtime after she showered.

A duplicate set of the clothes to what she wore, was beside the shower stall. Her sweaty clothes were to go into a canister in the corner. When she deposited them and closed the lid, they disappeared with a "Woop" sound.

The instructions on the wall explained the absence of a towel by outlining the air-drying procedure. When washed and dried she noticed, beside the full-length mirror, was a small shelf holding a comb, a deodorant, and a tiny sample of one of the cologne's she used to wear. She added the perfume then preened for just a moment. On the way down the hall Mabel felt a lightness in her step she had forgotten. Was it only that morning, a few hours ago, that she had to be wheeled to the gym? *This is beginning to sound alright*, she thought but to do it she had to force down a bitterness that rose like gall in her throat.

Cameron, the weightbot, directed her to a place at the cafeteria setting that was now four tables pushed together. Two other places were set. She was in the process of sitting down when clones of Cameron entered with their charges. Mabel thought they looked like the others she had seen in the gym earlier. The self-introductions that followed proved her right.

"I'm Mabel," she said holding out a hand to shake.

"I'm Irene," said the woman who clasped it. Mabel turned to the man, holding her silhouette to him just a fraction.

"I'm Harold," said the man. "We saw you in the gym, did we not?"

"Yes," Mabel replied putting a lilt in her voice. Everyone sat down.

"I wonder what people do in this place besides eat and work out in the gym?" Mabel asked of the others.

"You will rest after lunch and then attend your current events lecture followed by vocational training introduction," said Cameron who had been standing beside the table, in perfect chorus with his companions. They backed up as new drinkbots arrived carrying plates of food and a beverage. Each person seemed to get the same menu. As the small machines retired from the room, so did Cameron and his crowd, leaving the three Relinked people to their meal.

The silence that followed was broken only by the sounds of food being eaten hungrily.

It was dinnertime that evening before Mabel met her tablemates again. It had been a whirlwind, and emotional overload that buried her, and she presumed them, that afternoon. She was barely able to eat. She didn't even bother to clarify what each might have heard.

"So, the country is under martial law and we're part of the ruling class. We can live on DL reservations, but we have to work to stay here, and we have to choose the job we want to train for from a list – before breakfast. Did I leave out anything important?"

"We have two more days to complete our rehabilitation, I was told," Harold offered. "I think that was part of the barrage. By day after tomorrow, we move out to full-time training at some facility. Did they tell you where?"

"Not me. What about you Irene?"

"I think I slept through most of what they said. I don't recall being so tired since I was cutting eighty-hour weeks at work." She spoke into her bowl, hardly able to raise her head.

"I don't know what they put in these drinks," Harold held up the last of his before slurping it down. "I don't ache like I used to after a full morning at the gym."

Irene raised her head from staring down. Here was a tired face but an intellect that was squeezing out from under the routine that had been imposed on them. "Do you know anything about this place? Like where are we? How big is this place? How many others are here? Have you noticed there is nothing written, that isn't nailed to the wall? I used to be a corporate exec. This is what we invented to control imagination – work people to exhaustion then bombard them with talk."

The door to the hallway slid open and one of the Cameronbots led the other two into the room. "You can now review your vocational options and research tasks in your rooms," said one, for all. "Bedtime will be in two hours."

Irene cut off Cameron with a question. "Stop Cameron," she ordered. "Show me a map of this facility on your screen and where we are on it."

The robot paused seeming to process the request. A map appeared on the screen on its chest showing their adjacent rooms, the gym and the dining area along the corridor. "Set that map within a map of the whole facility," ordered Irene in the voice she'd use to make a dog sit.

"This is the map I have," the robot replied mechanically and refreshed the screen with the same map as before.

"Show me details of your map," Irene said.

A collection of diagrams flashed across the screen. They showed the placement of gym equipment, tables in the dining area in a variety of settings, their identical sleeping rooms with furniture located on a floor plan.

Irene raised her eyes again to catch the attention of Harold and Mabel in turn. "I think it is research time," she said meaningfully to the others. "See you in the morning." She set her hands on the arms of her chair and lifted herself up slowly. Her Cameronbot moved protectively to her side so she could lean on him.

"Cameron, I'd like more of that drink, and some water. Can you get it for me?" Irene asked.

A drinkbot appeared before she could get to the door to the hall. "Wow. That was fast. Did you see how fast they responded?" Irene turned as she made her observation. Mabel realized she'd been timing the exercise.

"How fast do the little guys move, Cameron?" Irene asked.

All three Camerons replied in unison. "Top speed is point eight metres per second."

Mabel found she could do the calculation immediately. The robots moved at less than fast walking speed. It hadn't taken more than ten seconds to appear. There should be a service doorway about ten metres away. Harold and Mabel followed Irene into the hallway. Lights only came on in the section they were in. Both caught Irene's hand wave and turned to scan the walls in the direction she indicated.

"Eleven o'clock on left," said Harold.

"Bedtime is nine thirty and your room is on the right, Harold," his Cameronbot corrected.

Mabel flashed a glance in the direction Harold had mentioned and saw the shadowed outline of a doorway in the wall, but it was not man-sized. The covered opening looked more like a doggy door from long ago to let the pet in and out of the kitchen. *Of course*, she thought. *Look who it's made for.*

Mabel stepped into her room and the door slid closed behind her. Her Cameronbot said "Good night, Mabel." As the door closed, Mabel heard the hum of Cameron's motors taking him away. She caught the door just before it closed and looked back into the hall. Cameron and his buddies were just entering the gym.

She toed off her slipper when she saw the drinkbot loaded with their dirty dishes coming out of the dining area. It motored past her headed for the hatch they had spotted. Leaving her slipper in the doorway to keep the door open, she stepped quickly in pursuit of the bot. The panel slid sideways and the machine entered. Mabel ducked down, caught the door and crawled partway through. Light from the hallway showed a Cameron-sized dispensing machine before her with an array of spigots. To left and right a tunnel, double bot width, stretched into darkness. She could hear humming that sounded like other robots in the distance. Bot dumped the dishes into a hopper, its serving space was sprayed and noisily blasted with air. Then the bot parked itself beside the dispenser. The panel through which she had crawled was bumping her like an annoyed elevator door. Mabel backed out and stepped quickly back to her room. Her own door was doing the same bumping thing against her slipper. Cameron appeared from the gym.

She snatched up her slipper and was leaning one-footed against the wall when the machine rolled up to ask what was wrong. "Stubbed my toe on the frame," she replied. But I'm OK. Just had to check my foot."

"Let me see," demanded Cameron. An articulated appendage like a retractable arm extended from a port in Cameron's body. It was warm and soft against her skin. Cameron told her to lean against the wall and lifted her foot in front of his screen. "You are not injured," it concluded, after a moment.

"Thanks Cam. I just had to check." Mabel replied.

"So did I. Goodnight Mab," replied the robot.

Mabel could not help but smile as she stepped into her room and the door slid closed behind her. She'd get at the terminal to see what jobs they would train her for. It had been a long time since she worked in an office and that just brought back the cruel joke George had played on her. Her smile faded into tight lips. The computer screen brightened at her approach and showed a "collection of questions to answer to narrow your choices to those best suited to your abilities," the screen said.

Mabel slouched back in her chair wondering if her eyes had become square. If her body needed the gym to come back to normal, her eyes seemed to need equivalent exercise and staring at a screen was not it. She pushed back and headed to the tiny shower that was part of her en suite facilities. She stripped while reading the instructions and tossed her sweaty clothes into the unit in the corner. It immediately 'Wooped' the garments away as soon as she closed the lid. At the same time a slot opened beside the unit and a shelf extended bearing identical garments to what had disappeared. She reasoned these were those she had taken off earlier after being washed. So, she had two sets of clothes. Hmmmm.

The shower had a wand that ejected needle thin sprays of water and soap, but it was strangely soothing and invigorating. The small amount of water that collected at her feet did not go down a drain. It sounded like it was vacuumed up. The wand even reminded her to run it over her head. When it was satisfied, she was clean enough, it announced the drying cycle would begin and jets of dry warm air blasted her skin. When dry, she set the wand back into the socket where it would serve as a faucet for the sink.

She had fallen into bed in the buff under a sheet. The room lights had faded, and she was drifting into sleep when she started up to retrieve her clothes. Up came the lights and she staggered across the room to move them to the chair by the bed. If they were her originals, she noticed the yogurt stains were gone. Her last thought as she collapsed back onto the bed was that she'd better like that coloured top because it seemed she was going to see a lot of it.

That moment before first sleep came back to her at lunch two days later. She was looking down at her top – the same one she'd been wearing for three days. It made her feel strange that in her earlier life, this would never have happened. She'd wear at least three outfits a day and spend much of the time between changes, wondering what to put on next. As she looked at the drying sweat stains, she realized she was noting them with a detachment and indifference she had never experienced.

Maybe it was the focus on the bodybuilding. When all you do is sweat and grunt all day, who has mental effort to devote to wardrobe? Maybe it was her social contacts –the robots. Now Cam was as amiable as she imagined a mechanical man could be. He had nothing else to talk about except the next exercise. He obviously monitored her physiological state closely, ordering up those supplemental drinks, which she had to admit, really revived her and kept her going. But he was still just a post on wheels with all the attraction thereof. Now Harold – he had potential.

But he was just as smelly, well smellier than she was, and Irene was slower coming up to speed. That's not true. Irene was the intellectual. She was the one that started them exploring their space. Irene asked the right questions. They had only figured out that they were in a big space like a hotel. Harold figured that out from looking at the maintenance records that he got into under the guise of looking for a vocation. Based on power usage, and heating costs, he figured out they were in something like a medium-sized hotel – probably a couple hundred 'guests'. *How come they never met any of them?* Mabel wondered. *That was a puzzle.*

They shared their vocational short lists over lunch. Harold wanted back into banking, but he found that banking has been nationalized. Well, not really. It turned out that the banks he recalled had now merged into a single entity sanctioned by the government – The Royal Bank of the Dominion of Canada. "Everybody got his oar in on that one, eh?" he summarized.

Further scrutiny after exercising all day led Harold to the conclusion that the business world was overwhelmingly dominated by a few corporate conglomerates who seemed to keep the illusion of states alive to give them cover. "Maybe this is why nationalizing has happened in most of the world" he suggested as he spoke. "Or is it the the nations of the world have all become corporatized - paper entities kept alive by mega-corporations.

"States have responded to threats of outside competition by banning anybody else from doing business in their country. So, the nations of the world each painted themselves into a corner, isolated from all the others, except for debating circles. The bridges between the nations are the conglomerates and they pave the pathways and finance the projects they wanted built. So, the banking business to which he aspired to return wasn't a competitive thing at all. It's a monopoly," he announced with some finality.

He went onto elaborate on other things he had found in his searching. The brazen side of the business world was revealed when he went looking for lists of the board of directors of the mega corps. He found members from one served on Boards of the other conglomerates. So, there were interlocking directorships. And who ran the countries? Well, it was political parties financed by the same conglomerates. Indeed, he rhymed off several heads of state, whose names meant nothing to the women, who were on those very Boards of Directors. "Hmmmph," he concluded.

"And by the way, want to guess the name of the top trans-national company in the world right now? DL Inc. It passed Apple like it was standing still. Their financial statements are columns of numbers under headings that say that those numbers below should be multiplied by a Trillion Dollars!"

"What mystifies me is the one opening listed that wants hundreds of people. In this world of computerized everything, why do they want so many people in "Asset Management'? How come the computers can't manage their assets?" Harold asked.

Irene hadn't said a word throughout Harold's monologue. She just kept chugging down her food is small bites and then finally polishing the plate with a crust of bread. When Harold finally stopped, she said into the silence that followed his question. "Asset Management" might not be what you think it means and/or there is something going on that computers can't figure out. I would bet there is a class of people not belonging to the mega-corps who are getting restless. Have you found anything about anyone not in one of those companies? Any news of festivals or rock concerts. When we delinked, there were wars all over the place. Have they gone out of style? Has peace broken out?"

I was drawn to the Environmental options," Mabel said, ignoring Irene's question. "It sounds like beaches and forests. There is a huge demand for Environmental Assessment officers. When you said that the title of the job might not be what I thought it was, Irene, it makes me wonder what is so complicated about the environment that it needs so many people to assess it?"

"I'm looking at Autonomous maintenance and repair," Irene said. "As you said for each of your main choices, there are a huge number of openings. Something is leading to a lot of breakdowns or what the robots are designed to do doesn't need doing any longer. So, what has changed or is changing?"

Only one Cameronbot arrived after their lunch to announce that their lesson time on current events would be taken up with their movement to their permanent quarters.

"Good News, Cam," Mabel replied. "I was thinking that my future was an endless treadmill. Let me go and pack my suitcase."

"I do not understand the word," Cameron replied.

"It's a joke, Cam. I have this one outfit and a duplicate." She pulled out the neckline. "I'm waiting to go shopping. Has the limo arrived?"

The robot stood silent.

"He probably doesn't know those words or concepts," Irene said. "But it looks like we're moving out. We must be fit."

A food bot appeared with three pairs of ear-covering earphones on its tray. A green light glowed on each pair. "You need to put these on then follow me," Cam directed.

As they walked along the hallway, Irene suggested, "Let's try to stay together when we get where we're going." Mabel was surprised to find she could hear Irene clearly despite the ear coverings.

"Right," both replied.

At an elevator, they rode upwards three floors emerging into a hallway brightly lit by a window wall looking out onto a lake. As soon as she saw it, Mabel recognized the lake and the cliff beyond. They were probably one floor down from the lounge where she had sat contemplating George's demise and chatting with, who was it, another lady about caring for … she couldn't recall. But she suddenly felt like she could put herself on a map of the place.

The windows faced east. It was only reflected sunlight that was coming in the window, but it seemed super bright. It was probably yet one more upgrade her body was going through. She remembered baby's squinting. Maybe newborns took a while to get used to the light. "Wow, that's bright," she said to the others. They too were shading their eyes even though they couldn't help looking out at the vista.

If the light was bright, the space was loud. Mabel made to remove her ear coverings and only lifted one before she slapped it back in place. "Don't take off your ear protectors," she warned the others. "It's really loud out there." Of course, Harold lifted his to check and quickly put them back on. "I wonder how we can hear each other so clearly in the midst of such noise?" Mabel asked.

"They remind me of ear protection you could get back in the day,"

Harold added. "There is some sort of tiny computer under that light that lets in some sounds and cancels others. Stands to reason though. If we each have new ears and we haven't heard anything louder than our own grunts, or Cam's instructions, maybe we have to go through some sort of sound resistance training."

The exchange and view out the window had distracted them. Cam's voice sounded in their earphones – polite but insistent. "Follow me, … Please," the voice said, and they turned to see he was waiting by an open doorway down the hallway to their left.

"I know where we are," Mabel announced to the others.

6

"Upstairs from here is where we came in before we Delinked," Mabel declared as they walked along the hall to the doors ahead. "We had a room in a tower just above here. If you go up one level, there's a lounge."

Cam led them through double doors into a wide hallway with a window wall on their right through which other people with yellow ear protectors could be seen on a wide balcony beyond. Some wore their ear protection up on their skulls above their ears; others were still in place. The vista was almost the same as the view earlier at the elevators but wrapped around to look northwards as well as to the east. Inside, the curving hall opened onto ranks of seats descending in an Amphitheatre arrangement that could probably seat three hundred.

They had a moment to look about. People. Other people! There were really others like them. Mabel couldn't keep her eyes still. She found herself assessing them. They all looked young – definitely nobody was old enough for wrinkles. They all seemed to be moving like kids learning to walk. No. More like teens who weren't quite used to their bodies. *Gangly might be a better word*, she thought *Probably that's what I look like.* People seemed to stay in the clumps they came in. They, too, were rubbernecking about like kids in a candy store. It struck her as strange when she realized it, that she hadn't paid any attention to what they were wearing – the first thing she remembered doing in her other life. *Hmmmph.*

More people were arriving in small groups with a supervising droid. All wore earphones. A soft chime drew attention and an invitation to find a seat sounded in their earphones. Groups chose spots away from each other – like paint spatters. When everyone was seated, they filled about half the ranked seating. The Cameronbots lined the auditorium on the floor at the top of the seating.

"The look like they could be the monoliths on Easter Island." Irene said, drawing attention to the crescent above them. "Someone should give them faces." The comment reminded Mabel of the lack of anything to write with. No pens, pencils, paints, crayons. She was going to say so, but a greeting interrupted her. "Hmmph," she said instead.

"Good afternoon," said a melodious voice in their ears. It seemed to be coming from a real person on the stage in front of them. He was trim, tanned and was wearing khaki long pants and a rich blue … what was that open-necked short-sleeved knit shirt … Golf shirt. *That's it*, she thought.

"Good afternoon and welcome to your new life," the speaker said. "I know some of you and maybe you remember me from your other life. My name is Brian. I know I don't look a day over eighty." He chuckled to himself. The audience was slow on the uptake.

"You will be moving into the training and socializing phase of your relinking," Brian said as though he was announcing some scandalous gossip that only they would know. He elaborated on how their workout programs would happen in large groups and would move on to team sports later. Training would be in classrooms now, again as part of the social program.

When he came to describing the apartments they would inhabit, he could scarcely contain himself. "They're a luxurious twelve square metres," he revealed with rising excitement, "with every space-saving, feature. You will love them, and they come with full bragging rights." Pictures flashed across the screen behind him. Mabel found herself staring numbly at the pictures unable to grasp what he was so excited about.

"Our dining complex is a network of coffee shops, restaurants, and bars situated adjacent to the promenade. We cater to every interest," he gushed. A floor plan appeared on the screen showing a space that might have housed a trade show broken by a tangle of walls reminiscent of a medieval streetscape. "Each eating area serves twenty-five or thirty diners," Brian bragged. "You can order when you arrive from the menu on the screen at each place, or from your room earlier and have it served immediately on your arrival. Food is not served in apartments," Brian added as an afterthought.

"Evenings are open for social activities at the theatres, in the sports park when team contests happen, or in our various library, workshop or research work areas." Brian concluded. "Any questions?"

The silence of information overload descended on the group till one voice called out, "Where's the shopping?"

A murmur ran through the group as though they too had just thought of that important detail.

"Along the promenade," pictures appeared on the screen to show boutiques the size of fitting rooms. "We have our various emporiums," Brian responded. "In these days, all items are purchased on-line. What you see here are the places where you and a few friends could gather to review a catalogue." A collage of different garments appeared quickly on the screen. "After you have made a selection and been scanned to ensure your items will fit perfectly, the item will be delivered to your apartment or if you wait, it can be created while you drink a beverage there or nearby. The cost of items must fall within the limits you established when you Delinked, of course."

"Can we travel?" asked another voice from the crowd.

"Travelling is individually arranged if you enter the request on your room screen."

Silence descended on the room.

"Hearing no more questions, I'll let you explore your new spaces. Your droid will accompany you to your living quarters and be sure you can find your way about the complex. You can then dismiss it or keep it till it is no longer needed." With that announcement, Brian turned and walked off stage. Everyone sat for a moment as though confused about what to do next.

Irene leaned across Mabel and Harold before they could rise from their seats. "I think we should plan to meet at least every night after dinner at the window wall or on the balcony out there," she hooked her thumb, "if the weather permits. We might meet during the day, but I think it would be good to have a place and time to talk when we don't have to follow someone else's directions. There is something about this place that sounds too good. What do you think?"

"Good idea," both agreed. Mabel also had that puzzled, questioning feeling bubbling up from the past that had made her look at tags when prices seemed too good. Groups were climbing to the top of the Amphitheatre and meeting Cameronbots there. There was no mixing of groups that Mabel saw.

"Did those people get the same Camerons they came with?" Irene asked our Cameron.

"We are all the same," was the robot's reply. "We each know you all and share everything you do.

"I meant the physical object. Are you the droid who brought us here from our lunchroom a while ago?"

"Of course."

"He's not you know," murmured Harold. "I left a ketchup fingerprint on ours. That's him with that group there." He nodded to a nearby cluster. They could see the small smear on the top.

"Does this sound like the Borg and hive mind and all that?" asked Irene.

"What's are Borgs?" asked Mabel. Harold and Irene shared an eyeroll and headshake.

"Maybe later," Harold suggested as they followed Cameron along the hall.

7

It was seven days before all three met on the deck as they had arranged. They all stood leaning on the railing looking out over the lake and the cliff beyond, sun setting at their back. On the intervening days, there had been only two or none of their group. They were all relieved. It wasn't that they had been isolated – quite the contrary. At every turn they bumped into others who were all too anxious to make their acquaintance. "It's a bit like a real-time social media thing," Irene summarized. "It is almost a duty or at least expected that you greet everyone by name as you pass. I think medieval villages must have been like this – except there are no kids here."

"I was going to say it is like one of those adult resorts I remember – hordes of self-indulging gorgeous people everywhere you go," added Mabel. "I was one of them, strutting my stuff and looking for another fling. That is what mystifies me. I see nobody making a pass at anyone, even me. It isn't that there aren't enough unattached and eligible candidates. I just don't find myself excited by any of them. I wondered if they are magazine pictures just walking around."

Mable looked out over the lake and said to the space, "How could that happen that so many should be walking around bumping into each other without the slightest interest in a roll in the sheets together?"

Harold felt like his friend was propositioning him. "Tell me about the job you chose to train for," he asked to divert her interest.

"See," said Mabel nudging Irene. When Irene just shrugged, Mabel decided to answer the request. "Well, that has been an eye-opener. It's only been a week but the Environment that is being assessed is not the beaches and parks I imagined. I think what they want people to measure is the Human Environment – like all these people around us. I think that Environment Assessment Officers – EAO's if you can believe the creative acronym – are actually modern-day cops! That's what takes up most of the management chart. There is a piece on the edge that seems to suggest EAO's might deal either with immigration or forest fires or floods or storms – stuff like that.

"Interesting," Harold replied. "I was coming to the same conclusion about what names mean. I signed up for Asset Management and couldn't figure out why people were needed to do accounting jobs. Well, they don't want bean counters. I think the world is so computer-integrated that algorithms have come to the point where they don't know what to do with anything random. So, I've been trying to imagine random events and come up with - like weather events, asteroid impacts, lightning bolts – hardly what would tilt a bank's balance sheet. The only thing I am left with is a big factor of unknown composition. War comes to mind, but I haven't found anything about who might be fighting a war or where.

"How many places are there like this one?" asked Irene.

Both looked at her as though she was talking to another group.

Both shrugged. "Where did that question come from?" Mabel asked.

"Well, I listen to both of you say that there seems to be new names for jobs we knew by other names and that says this," she waved her hand around them, "has to be either an isolated colony or a part of a larger structure with the power to create these odd names.

"I'd say this is only one of many places like it," Mabel offered. "The number of people being sought to fill the jobs I'm enrolled to pursue demands a much larger collective.

"I agree," Irene said. "I put in for Autonomous Maintenance and Repair. Only a bit of the job seems to be nuts and bolts stuff. What I see on my horizon is computer code, program design, and hacking protection.

Nobody has mentioned hacking but when they talk about tight code and creating computer firewalls now, they make the last ones I knew look like tissue, I wonder who is trying to get in?"

They turned to look out over the lake, now sinking into shadow. The moon was peeking over the horizon to the southeast. "A place this size needs a huge amount of food and waste management. Tell me what you think about the food."

"Delicious," Mabel answered and went on until the moon rose, with her evaluation of the week's menus.

Irene snapped her fingers. "I'll bet that answers your question about why nobody is making a pass at you," Irene answered when Mabel finally stopped.

"What?"

"I'll bet the food is 'fortified' not only with every vitamin known but also with enough endorphins or drugs to keep everybody happy and celibate."

Mabel slapped her chest in shock. "Do you think? Is that possible?"

"Makes sense to me," Harold added. "If it was so, it might explain the anomalies we've mentioned. Within our group everybody is smiley and sociable but there are no contests, battles for supremacy. So, while everything is kept copacetic on the home front, there is a group who might not be at the happy table – like a large bunch of people outside places like this."

"Do you mean that our very behaviour is being jerked around by what we're eating?" Mabel was shocked to the core.

"That might be why you have to show your wrist ID for each meal. The dose you get is individualized."

"My God," Mabel exclaimed. And then she added with a slap of her hand on the railing. "You're right! Absolutely right! In my earlier life, nothing was more important that my wardrobe – well after my body." She ran her hands down the curves she so admired. "My closet then was bigger than my apartment now. But since I've been here, I haven't hankered to look at a single fashion magazine. I must be on drugs to keep that from happening. And because my clothes get washed or cleaned or renewed or something every time, I take them off, my current wardrobe consists of one daywear set and one for dinner and after. The whole thing would fit in a file folder. What is mystifying me is why I don't even care."

"Remember you found the hatch through which the drinkbots entered?" Irene asked. I haven't seen anything like that this week. We all go for our meals. Even the Cameronbots have disappeared."

"I'll bet they're tending to a new bunch of Relinks."

"Too soon," Harold offered. "My guess is that we must be out of the training facility before the new batch of relinks appears. From what I see, we've got a couple more weeks, or months, to be turned into what they want - whoever 'they' are. He did double hooks in the air.

Irene interrupted again. "I was talking to one of the people who has chosen to serve in the restaurants. She was saying that when you order food at her place, the meal you want comes out of something that looks like an old vending machine. It has your own name on it when it emerges, all hot and steaming. They take the label off before it goes to the table.

"Are you saying that the vending machine is really some sort of kitchen or cooler and microwave combo."

"I like that," Irene replied, "and if you were to get your sedatives or whatever, it could be added to the meal right at that point."

"I wonder if they make up picnics to take on a walk?" Mabel asked.

"Try, why don't you."

"Hmmmph. I might just do that."

"Well look whose here," Harold observed. A Cameronbot was coming through the doorway onto the balcony.

"It is time for you to sleep," it observed mechanically.

"We were just standing out here hoping you would come and get us, Cam. Nice to see you again, old buddy. How you doing?" greeted Mabel.

"It is time for you to sleep Mab," the machine replied.

"OK," Irene replied. "We're coming." She headed towards the door but turned back to murmur, "Keep the faith and the time, guys?"

"Yep," they said in chorus.

*

"The Cameronbots are the gophers," Irene reported four days later, "and I have managed to make up an identity code that makes me look like one to the others. I wrapped it over my own bracelet, and they completely ignored me. I've been doing a little exploring down the service tunnels. They're not well lit and that map of the premises you got me Mabel doesn't even show a pair of double doors that won't open but seem to be the access to a space under a large chunk of this building."

"Why wouldn't the door open if you had a droid identity?" asked Mabel.

"You won't believe this, but it had a lock that opens with a key."

"I was standing there when a Cameronbot came by, and it was as though I wasn't even there. He zipped right past. I've been thinking about that since. Remember how he didn't know what we meant when we asked him for a map of the place and all he had was the route he followed with us from the gym to the dining room to our cells when we Relinked?"

"I am interested to find that there is a gap in the historical record of assets being managed," Harold burst in to change the subject. "It is as though a whole new operating system was created just about the time I Delinked. My guess is that it had to do with the Quantum Computers that had just come into being."

Mabel wanted to pick up on Irene's comment. "Harold, I don't want to be rude but give me a chance to respond to Irene." She stopped with her fingers to her lips as though the words had come out unbidden. "In my old life, I can't ever recall worrying about what anyone else felt. Sorry Harold but I need to answer Irene's question. I do remember Cam's inability to imagine anything but what he'd been programmed to do. I'll bet he wouldn't see a door he wasn't programmed to recognize either. Hmmmph." She thought of the locked door for a moment as she looked out the window wall into a gentle rain that was keeping them inside. "So back to you Harold. What's this about a new computer operating system?"

"Well, it is just that the records I can access, like Assets portfolios and money exchanges that happened just after the time I delinked. I've asked the computer for data before that, and it says there is none. Well, I know that DL Inc existed then, I can't believe it didn't keep records. I had to give over everything I owned as did everyone else. But if they were on computers whose operating system isn't part of the new reality, it might just be a closed book to this system. I expect they might have created new, collected accounts for the new system but the record of whose assets went into them might not be available now. Not that it matters because the money or whatever would be moved around to maximize profit anyway. It is just I was curious to see if I could find when and for how much they sold my condo."

Harold's words brought back something to the edge of memory, but not across that barrier, for Mabel. "I can't quite remember a conversation that I had with my husband – God curse his soul – just before we delinked. I was planning to ... not delink, but he said something that really ticked me off. What the Hell was it he said?"

"I wonder if you know how to pick a lock, because if you knew maybe we could see what's behind the double door. Would you be up to giving it a try tomorrow night?"

"Sure," replied Mabel. "The movie they are playing in the theatre tomorrow night was no good when it was first made. It hasn't improved with time. But you know you need something thin and bendable to slide into the lock to hold up the pins so you can turn the barrel." Mabel suggested. "It was one of the skills I learned in my adolescence – when – a hundred years ago?"

Both women laughed. Irene withdrew two pins from her long hair. "I typed in a request for a bobby pin to hold my hair in place. And this is what was delivered. She handed over the metal clips with a blob of something covering the sharp ends. With a fingernail, Mabel scraped the pin clean. "We have to straighten that crimping so it is flat," she said.

Harold looked at the pin and bent the fold-over straight. It gave him a long metal finger with wrinkles on each end. He stuck one end into the narrow slot between the metal door and its frame. He levered sideways slightly, and the pin straightened the first crimp. He pushed the tip further into the doorframe and bent the other way and the next bend was corrected. Irene gave Mabel the one she held and pulled another from her hair. They each went to work at different doors making what they hoped could pick a twentieth century lock in the twenty-first.

"I have to practice with my team tomorrow," Harold said, "but I can be here night after next."

"See you then," the women said.

*

Mabel had been at her task for ten minutes – it seemed much longer. Her fingers were sore trying to manipulate the tiny flat wires. "I have to lift those pins in the lock so the barrel can rotate and open the lock," she explained. "I can feel four going up out of the way, but it is the last two that I can't move."

Their efforts were disturbed by a sound approaching.

"Just back out of the way and let it pass," Irene said and drew her tight against the tunnel wall opposite the doors. "You have a bot code on. It won't even stop," Irene predicted. The Cameronbot didn't even change speed as it hummed past. Mabel let out a sigh as it disappeared into the gloom.

"It's because of the angle, I think," Mabel eventually sighed. "My pin is way into the lock, so I have little room to wiggle. And the lock likely hasn't been opened in fifty years so it's stiff … plus the fact that I'm sadly out of practice. I'm afraid I'm stuck."

They backed away from the door to let another robot pass. As she did, Mabel glanced up at the ceiling and another thought came from a shady past.

"That's a drop ceiling," she said. "There should be a space above those tiles for wires and ductwork."

"So what," Irene whispered.

"Well, if that wall with the door is just a curtain wall and not needed to hold up the floor above, there might be a space to get over it and into the other side of that door."

"Really?" Irene was processing the image that came of a workman standing on a ladder in her office an age ago. His head was poked up through exactly such tiling and wires were dangling down through the hole.

"Here," said Mabel. "You're lighter. Let me boost you up." She cupped her hands for Irene to step into and hoisted the woman up the wall.

Irene pushed at a panel, and it popped up out of the metal track that suspended it – and immediately bumped into something that let out a slight "boom". "That's ductwork, Mabel interpreted." Come down and we'll try the next tile." It popped up and Irene pushed it onto the supports beside it.

"There is space up here," she said.

"OK," Mabel coached. "Can you grab anything to pull yourself up? Step up onto my shoulders. I'll guide your feet. Step on the metal framing of the panels. If you put your weight on a panel it will collapse.

"Yeah, I can see the edge of a duct and the wall just goes above the ceiling but not to the next floor above. OK. Let's see if we can do this." Mabel hoisted Irene up to stand on her shoulders. "I can see a handhold. Can you push my feet up with your hands?" A humming indicated the approach of a robot.

"One chance. Go," and she pressed up with all her strength. A cascade of grit and dust fell over Mabel's head. Irene's weight immediately came off Mabel's outstretched arms and disappeared through the hole. Mabel sank back against the wall to let the bot by, fighting to hold her breath.

Irene's smiling face peeked down through her tangled hair as soon as the bot was gone.

"If it is the way I recall, the room will have a plaster or panelled ceiling you can kick or break right through. It will be held up about every sixteen inches but there is room for someone slim like you to drop down through if you can kick the ceiling down," Mabel hissed. "Look for a light switch beside the door."

Irene's face disappeared. A few minutes later, Mabel thought she could hear a thumping. That was the failure in their plan, it occurred to her. Irene might be light enough to lift up, but she didn't have the weight to break through the other ceiling. The thumping quit then started again. "Ineffectual," Mabel concluded. She was just about to call out to Irene when the pounding renewed but this was louder. A tearing followed each bump. A crash followed and coughing then quiet. Mabel pressed her ear to the door, straining to hear anything. That was where she was when the door opened suddenly, and she lurched into the room. It was like falling into a cooler.

The next sensation, after the cold, was that it was really bright – daytime bright from ranks of overhead banks of lights. The third impression was that the place was huge, filled with metal shelving units. Irene jerked her all the way into the room and quickly closed the door.

Mabel staggered to her feet looking around. She turned to her disheveled collaborator dusting down her clothes and trying to pull back her unruly tangled hair. "Yes," Irene said. "Wonderful things."

Mabel looked about. "I think someone else got that line earlier. Wow! Look at this place!" she exclaimed softly she stared off into what looked like a repurposed gymnasium filled with shelving laden with suitcases.

She looked back at Irene. "What's that?" Mabel asked pointing to the huge scissors at her feet.

"I found them on top of the ductwork. I'll bet a workman left them there, last century and at the end of the day he just put in for a new pair of tin snips because he couldn't find those. Anyway, it was just the thing to punch through the ceiling. As you said it is plaster, but I couldn't break it without the pointy things."

The adrenalin high of the last half hour was beginning to take its toll. Mabel slid down the wall to sit against it on the floor. The cold was getting to her also. Plumes of breath billowed into the still air.

"What is this place?" Mabel asked. "It looks like the lost and found at an airport."

Irene got up to walk across the end of the room. Faded labels marked each shelf along the end.

"Do you recall your married name before you delinked?" she called.

"Reluctantly, why?"

"Do you remember the date you delinked?"

I remember the day my husband dumped me into this never-never land was in February. It could have been 2020. Why?"

Irene had disappeared down an aisle. When Mabel caught up, Irene was hauling a suitcase off a shelf over her head. Mabel caught it as it came loose. "I delinked about that time too and you know what, here's the suitcase I brought here."

As Mabel lowered the case to the floor, the thought she could not recall last night clicked over the threshold into consciousness.

"How did you find this?" she asked hardly daring to hope.

"I think the code on the end of the aisle is a month and year. The days are in order starting at that end." Mabel had already spun away. Irene opened her case and squeaked in delight at finding favourite jewelry.

As soon as she passed the first aisle, she knew she was going the wrong way. She spun around and found the year and month of her event. She was three steps down the aisle and looking onward, when she saw them.

Those monster cases could only be hers and George's. The keys and a tag were tied to the top handle. "Mabel Twilling," it read. She stepped past and hauled it into the aisle. Yanking on the cord holding the keys cut her hand before it broke. She trembled with the key to open the latch and the sides swung open. It was jammed with her dresses, jackets, pants, discoloured from time and perspiration likely. She pulled the drawers of underwear and stockings out of their tracks and ran her hand along the lining at the back. "Yes!"

With the nail file from the cosmetic case, she stabbed through the tender lining and ripped downward. With her fingers in the tear, she yanked sideways and there it was – a weighty curtain. Into each padded square like blocks on a quilt was her emergency hoard of gold coins. The whole padded piece was attached to the lining itself. It was the thirty-thousand-dollar emergency fund. And… she yanked the tear the other way to reveal two tubes, each about the size of her finger and three times as long. She slid it from its holster and shook it. "YES!" she shouted.

"Did you find your suitcase?" Irene asked as she came around the end of the aisle and headed towards her.

"Indeed, I did," Mabel replied. Quickly she slid the drawers back into place. "These were my favourite pieces of jewellery," she said holding up a jade necklace and another of many pieces of amber. She slid that drawer closed.

"You know we can't take this stuff out there," Irene held up her own glittering necklace, "until we figure out a few other things. Wearing these things is only one problem. Technically it belongs to DL Inc. But because it's here, my guess is that they don't even know it. As far as they are concerned these are lost goods. But I don't know if I could claim finders-keepers," she said. "All these cases were the ones brought by all those other people we're training with, and others besides, I'd bet. I wonder if they just got forgotten when the computers changed, as Harold said."

She's right, Mabel thought. *There is a fortune here and I have to leave it. Well at least we know what's in here.* "We'd better get back. It must be bedtime by now," Mabel added. Irene turned to return her necklace to her case. As soon as she rounded the corner and was out of sight, Mabel retied her suitcase keys to George's case and snapped hers closed. Nobody was getting into that without a rotary cutter and a wrecking bar.

They were at the door ready to leave when Irene said, "We have to lock this door. It won't do to have it bumped open by accident. Think of the confusion it would cause to those poor robots."

Mabel agreed. She was shivering now from either the adrenalin rush or the chilly air, she wasn't sure. They pushed over a table and set a suitcase on it under the hole. She stepped into the hall and the bolt clicked behind her. It felt so warm in the tunnel. In moments Irene's feet were dropping down through the ceiling, thrashing to find Mabel's hands. As soon as she was steadied on Mabel's shoulders, she slid the ceiling panel back in place and dropped to the floor.

"That was an adventure, wasn't it?" Irene suggested as they headed back down the service tunnel.

8

"I expect that appearing with something not on a list would probably precipitate a nervous breakdown in the computer system," Harold replied. They were meeting on the deck overlooking the lake.

"How about asking for a bunch of new clothes?"

"Your expense limit was determined when you delinked and paid up front. See anyone with new ones now? Why do you suppose that is – or isn't. Is everyone in the same financial boat?"

"It sure supports the drugged life-style theory. But let me ask another thing, Harold. Tell me about the money system. Why is it we don't have any money to spend? Why don't people go out anywhere? Do you know that if you ask to travel, they set you up for a virtual image helmet and charge you as though you went to that place when you haven't left the room. What a rip-off."

"I can only say that DL Inc. has such a large numbers on its balance sheet and income that the column is headed 10_{15} - that is the number in that column in quadrillions of dollars. When I delinked, Apple had just claimed the first company to be valued over a trillion dollars. The total income of the all the countries in the whole world was said to be just under a hundred trillion dollars. DL Inc is more than a thousand times bigger that that now. It bought Apple and all the other computer companies in the world for less than five percent of its gross annual income. DL Inc is financially bigger than the national income of almost all the countries in the world combined.

"That doesn't make sense. Why would countries exist if every one of their major businesses are owned by one conglomerate?" Irene scoffed.

"Maybe it is another form of drugged existence. Let people think they really run things, give them something trivial to do, like decide which movie to watch or what clothes are in fashion, and they really think they control their environment."

"That's another odd fact I turned up. In the early part of this century there were a hundred and ninety-three countries in the UN. Now there are hardly a hundred. Climate change might have submerged some island nations in the Pacific but where did half of them go? I asked for a map of the nations of the world, and I can't get one. So, I asked for the annual income of tropical countries like Kenya, Nigeria, Indonesia ..." He rhymed of a string. "They are not reported. Countries in the far latitudes have incomes but no nation in the tropics seems to have anything worthy enough to report. They appear to have virtually disappeared."

"Well, our news pales beside that," Irene said. "We found a storeroom full of the luggage of all the people who delinked just before the computer changeover you mentioned earlier. I found my suitcase and my mother's necklace. So did Mabel."

Harold's head snapped up. "Say what? You found the luggage of hundreds of people that we train with now?"

"Yes."

"Where?"

"Behind the doors Mabel went at with her hair pins. It's about the size of a tennis court, metal shelving, three shelves high, hundreds of suitcases, all arranged by date of delinking I think and all in the couple years before the Quantum Computers system took over and all behind an old-style key lock."

"Harold," Irene asked, "Why wouldn't that room full of suitcases be in the computer records? I have trouble with that."

Harold exhaled loudly through pursed lips. "Well, there is a fundamental reason why the Quantum computers can't link with the older ones. Quantum computers run on qubits that are units that have three possible states – plus, minus and both. The old computers could only run on and either-or frame. Each byte is either a one or a zero – no halfway or other way. So, the operating system that runs one isn't compatible with the other. But as for why that room of stuff got lost, could be much more mundane. I mean how many accounts got moved over one at a time. It could be that the programmer who was to do that went for lunch and his replacement started a couple lines further down the page."

"I wonder what's in all those cases?" Irene asked.

"Me too," said Harold. "Have you noticed how there is nothing here to write with – anything to make a personal note with? The only way to communicate is through the computer and that monitors everything. Do you suppose there'd be pencils in any of those cases? The ink in any pens would likely be hard now but pencils would work."

"I had a whole collection of eye-liner pencils. I'd hate to try to write an essay with one, but in the bottom of my collection there might be an old pencil. I know there should be one of those Swiss Army knives with all the blades, and the fold out snow shovel, in the bottom of my case."

"Fold out snow shovel? I don't remember one with that," Harold said puzzled.

"It's a joke, Harold. They seemed to have every other attachment, I just pretended they must have a shovel and probably a coffee maker too."

Harold blushed at being sucked in so easily.

"George had one too. He was Mr. Self-sufficient. You'd be surprised at how often you need a sharp blade or awl."

"Mabel has something there," Irene said. "I'll bet there are all sorts of things that would get us off the communication grid in those cases. There were laptop computers back then also weren't there?"

"We are talking about geriatrics remember. Some maybe had one. But they'd be battery operated. I don't know if they'd charge again after being so long out of use. But think what else there might be – nail files, nail clippers, prescriptions, … the mind boggles."

"George had a small tank of oxygen or two in the bottom of his trunk."

"I wonder if anyone had a gun?" Harold asked. "God that room could be an arsenal against conformity."

"I think that gives you some idea of the significance of that room. It is unknown now. What would a quadrillion dollar company do to eliminate anything it didn't control?"

"Well, the evidence is in the number of EAO's currently being trained," Mabel suggested. "What they'd do is everything to control it!"

"That puts us at the pointy end of a very big corporate problem."

"Are you well," asked a mechanical voice that had appeared without warning. "You seem very anxious, Irene." It was a Cameronbot.

Irene paused a moment. "Do you mean my forehead was wrinkled and I was frowning?"

"Yes."

"I was doing an exercise from back before we delinked. It's to limber up facial muscles. We spend so much time smiling here that we need to also exercise the opposing muscle groups that make us frown and balance the other ones. It is part of keeping healthy. Everyone should be doing it as part of their regimen. It is a flaw in your program not to recognize that need. I've been talking to others to get them to remember to exercise frown musculature."

Cam seemed unable to reply. "It is bedtime," it said.

"Nice catch, Irene," complimented Mabel as they headed to their rooms.

*

"We've been talking to a few others. We don't want to be attracting undue attention," Irene explained to Harold, "and we've been keeping a list."

"On paper?"

"I keep it in my sock."

"I requisitioned a book bag as you asked and got two heavy books from the library but I'm not sure what for." Harold said.

"Here comes the reason," Irene said looking past him at Mabel striding through the door onto the deck swinging an identical bag which she set down beside his but closer to his leg than the one already there.

"Good evening, all!" Mabel said cheerfully. "Midsummer night, did you know?" She bent to pull out a large coffee table book from the bag she had brought, laid it out on the wide railing and started pointing to it and where the moon would rise and different planets after that. Others nearby leaned over to catch a peek and look where she pointed even though the sky was still bright. "You have to wait until it gets dark to see the planets," she explained to the others.

"Don't know if I've ever seen a planet," said one and excused himself to go to the movies.

When they had some space, Mabel said, "we found three people who remember having iPads, laptops or smart phones they left in their luggage. We only spoke to a few. Most said they brought no luggage at all because they knew where they were going. Anyway, in the book bag are those items and we wondered if you could see if they can charge up. And before you ask, we did bring the chargers with them. It's just we don't know where to find an outlet that them might fit into."

"I'll see what I can do. On another topic, I have an idea about why we are being trained. I suspect we are the history books that the Qubit Computers don't have. I told you that there is a fundamental barrier between the systems, so we are the means by which the current regime connects to all that data that was stored in those binary systems. We remember them, or some of the stuff in them. By watching us they get what they need. I am interested to see the fallout from the scam you pulled on Cambot back a week or so ago."

"Do tell."

"In one of our training tasks we had to research financial trends, only since the Qubit Computers came into being, interestingly enough, and one of the ladies found a record of her son's death in a car accident. It was the end of a long article sort of added onto the business page from another. She followed it back and fell into tears when she recognized other names in the article. In the past, the Cambot would always respond by taking the tearful or frustrated or cursing anyone out of the room. In this case, the first question it asked was if she was exercising her frown muscles. Needless to say, that was even more off-putting."

"That is interesting," Irene replied and turned to stare out over the lake. "Clouds coming in," she observed after a period of thought. "Might not be much to see tonight."

"Let me refine a thought bit more," Harold offered. He had plainly not been listening. "Is it possible that the computing power that allowed DL Inc to exist, to offer people the ability to keep coming back time after time, requires a perpetuation, a stabilizing of history that never has happened before. Those people who come out of their cubes come with a collection of thoughts and behaviours that upset the applecart. Does DL Inc need people now to monitor and interpret behaviour of this random element in the partnership? The others thought while he drew a breath.

"People don't like another turn of the treadmill that would be really acceptable to a machine. People are the product of a series of changes, and it is bred into their bones to keep doing so. The machine is the product of control," and, he double bracketed in the air, "'seeks', the repetition and unchanging that it was built to create and maintain. Is that too philosophical to imagine - that we are between two forces – not of good and evil, but of change and stasis?"

"Well, I think you'd have to grant the property of imagination to the machine to do that. It would be a million-dollar, mechanical human. It would plan. It would have a soul."

"Why? The machine doesn't need a soul. It just needs to do over what it did before. I have a growing suspicion that DL Inc. is in a tussle with itself. It has sold people on 'coming back'. To what? To what they left! They wanted it over again, only younger. I think that is what I was expecting."

"I remember someone asked me, in an earlier life, what the purpose of life was. I think I replied, "to reproduce". But in reproducing, we created a baby that was different from any person ever born. Felt like reproducing lately? See anyone else in the family way? If a machine reproduces, what does it make? – Another one like itself – exactly."

"Imagine this Delink-Relinking happening in another period of history. The Neanderthals would expect to reappear as Neanderthals, not some effete, naked being who couldn't run down a deer or throw a spear. So, a machine that sold such a repeat existence would be committed to recycling their loop of history. If the Neanderthals who came back decided that they really wanted to mate with and harness the talents of those newbies on the block – Sapiens – then the machine controller that allowed them to return would need to stop that urge and harness their behaviours to controlling the process going backward or at least standing still."

Irene took a moment before she added. "I think that such a line would lead the machine to act to preserve what it was created and programmed to do and that deviants who threatened that process were really enemies of the state. People would be controlled biologically to meet the programmed objectives."

"And anyone that threatened that would need further training or find a target on their backs."

"I can smell the paint drying already. Check for me will you. Do you see an 'X' or a bullseye?" Irene turned her back to the others, then turned to face them again.

"I should have gone to the movies," Mabel lamented.

"Harold, have you been eating regularly? Did you get your three happy meals today?"

"As a matter of fact, I've been nibbling on that freeze-dried fruit cake you brought from the luggage room. It was a bit like nibbling a chair leg, but with a slug of water, it chewed up pretty well. I asked for meals at my desk this week so I could work on my assignment – like a good worker bee - but I didn't eat them. I dumped them in the toilet.

"My God Harold. All you do is make me sad I met you." Mabel groaned.

They all stood leaning on the railing looking out over the lake under the darkening, cloud-covered sky. "So, you going to see if you can charge up that equipment?" Mabel asked finally.

"Yeah."

9

"Well one, the iPad, took a charge and held it for a few hours of work. It had three thousand five hundred songs, mostly classical, and almost that number of indifferent photos going back over the years previous to delinking, I guess. That it revived at all suggests that it was not heavily used and that it was pretty cold for most of its life. Still, this is way past its planned lifetime. There were a few emails on it but I would guess the person was not an e-mailer, confirmed by the lack of any social media icons. He'd have been classified as an electronic hermit," Harold summarized. "I put the stuff on top of the ceiling panels in the gym dressing room."

"It raises the question of what good such stuff is anyway," he continued. "There might be some use as parts, but I have no idea whether that is even a rational thought. Parts to fix what? I would expect something so old is pretty obsolete." He let the thought settle. "And I'm back on syntha-food and feeling absolutely indifferent."

Mabel was wondering the same about the treasure in her suitcase. Gold and diamonds were only useful if someone wanted, really coveted them. And honestly, she couldn't wind herself up to care as she once had. There was that momentary thrill that she had somehow beaten some system, but so what. What she had was rare as moon rocks in this place, but so what? Who needed moon rocks?

Maybe it was the meal meds that made her so blasé.

"As long as we know that the-don't-give-a-damn feeling is not ours," said Irene to try to break the mood, "I can push it away to ask questions. I came up with something strange the other day. It was part of a repair course. We were each given a broken piece of equipment to repair by following a procedure on the screen. The instructor said that each piece had actually been in use within the complex." She snuggled into the blanket she'd brought from her bed to wear as a shawl. Despite it being mid-summer, it was cool. They hadn't seen the sun for a week.

"I got some sort of security monitor. The report said it had been hit by a falling branch found lying across it. I think it was programmed to take photos for some time period and then download them in a burst in response to a command signal. I remember things like this were called camera traps and were used to study wild animals. Anyway, this thing had taken a whale of a whack judging from the dint in the housing. The sharp edge of the dint had cut some wires inside and the lens was broken. I replaced the broken pieces but before I blanked the memory, I ran the pictures to be sure it worked properly. I think they were squirrels I was watching, at least one blue jay. Just before the screen went blank. I saw a picture of two people. Both were heavily bearded and pretty hefty specimens."

"Sasquatch," Harold interrupted.

Irene paused as though his comment had derailed a thought then continued as though he had said nothing. "There was only one frame and then the branch hit the unit. This is the chip with the picture. She held opened her palm secretively to show the small plastic box and its contents.

"All this stuff is old binary technology and I wondered whether you could connect it to the iPad or whatever to keep it. I logged into the repair record that it needed a new memory chip to complete the repair so I could put the unit back into inventory."

"Well, I might be able to store the picture, but I guess the question would be why?" Harold asked.

"Well, it proves there are others, and they are not in here. They're out there." Irene nodded out over the lake.

"You were saying that your financial searches made you wonder if DL Inc was fighting a war. Well maybe they are, and these are a scouting party. Or maybe they are just survivors from a distant time – the children of those who didn't get into here. I just don't think we should throw a way information like this because we can't figure out what use it is. I think that indifference is the dinner drugs talking."

With a sigh, Harold palmed the chip from Irene and slid it into his pocket. "You're right. I'll see if I can capture it."

Mabel, who had felt left out of the conversation, jumped into the pause. "Do you think there might be anything else in the luggage lock-up that we might use?"

"Well, we'd have to know what we wanted to do. I just have this big feeling of angst that something is wrong, and it's being hidden from me. All this calm and orderly feeling seems really contrived."

"In our training, we were offered a couple options – I guess like fixing real equipment in your program," Mabel offered. "They offered us a set of field trips to look at natural environments we might be assigned to assess. I expect it is flying over rocks and trees. What you've said suggests I should put my name down for that, at least for now. I'm not really interested in camping out. I did enough of that for two lifetimes, back then."

"That reminds me," Irene added. "When I was looking at the edges of the dint in the housing of that camera unit, there were small chips of rock in the break. There was no doubt. They were about sand sized but sharp and shiny. How would they come from a tree branch?"

"That sounds like a no-brainer," Mabel replied. "A rock fell on it and then the tree branch – like an avalanche."

"An avalanche that took out one camera and one tree branch and left everything else untouched," Irene said. "Yeah, it's a real no-brainer."

10

It's my scarf that really gives me away, she thought. She realized that as she sat on the log waiting for transport their instructor said would be arriving to take them on their first and much delayed, environmental outing. It was a vanity, she knew, but she had stuck to her guns and got it.

When she had moved from the re-link suite and found she could order clothes online, indeed could not get them any other way, she had asked for a scarf. A grey woolen strip of cloth as long as her arm and wide as her hand was delivered. Thus began her interactions with the machine world's 'Service Department'. It became progressively obvious that a machine had no idea what the term 'Service' meant.

If the grey excuse "was not appropriate, maybe she would like a brown one," the screen had asked and showed her that alternative - and every other variant in the database. She eventually was forced to enter design criteria for a health support garment that she thought were as complex as those required to construct a building. She had to specify size, material mix, elasticity, weave, compressibility, warmth coefficient, transparency, colours, edging - she lost track - but the result was the wonderful, material she now was twisting into a rope with which to tie back her hair. She set the knot to the side of her neck to-day; the ends trailed over her shoulder.

The gauzy material was a square the size of her outstretched arms. It could be twisted into a rope the width of her finger. Tension changed the colour of the fibre from a blood red to purple. When left flat it was an off-white. If she folded it in half, it worked as a shawl to wear on the balcony when she met Irene and Harold, or she could fold it lengthwise several times into a band to make into a turban or headscarf. She found a diagonal twisting would make it long enough for a belt or waist accent that changed colour along the fold lines. And the fabric was as tough as steel.

Others had asked her where she got it. "I just ordered it from the catalogue," she replied. When others persisted after they couldn't find it, she just shrugged and feigned ignorance. To get one, they would have to suffer the health issue to which she had attached the garment and they would not find out that disability from her lips. Not that many tried. When she wouldn't tell them, and it the scarf didn't turn up on the screen, most lost interest. Maybe it was the drugs in the dinner again.

Few people could recall her name now. She was 'the lady with the scarf', and here she sat on a log waiting for the drone to collect her, her instructor, and her two classmates for a tour of the area they were to assess as part of their training. The instructor was talking into a communicator seeking the machine that was not on the landing pad. When she sat down at the end of the log so the others could sit beside her, they chose to stand apart and discuss the movie they had seen the previous night, and which Mabel had not.

She had hardly settled on the log before the flies found her. They were tiny black things. At first few arrived then they seemed to descend in legions. Mabel flipped off her scarf and shook it out full size and draped it over her head like a tent. It was easily see-through but it was a barrier to the pests that beset her. Her companions were not so equipped. They were flailing the air fruitlessly, as was the instructor. Eventually he was told the drone they were assigned was in need of repairs and could not come that day. Before he could complete his sentence announcing the change in plans, the other two were running back to the building. Mabel retreated more gracefully.

It took three days of treatment for the fly bites to stop itching. Twice more they sat at the pad waiting for the drone that didn't come but on each of those days, everyone was steaming in hazmat suits that, while they were effective against the tiny black flies, were so stifled the students that the instructor called off the flight rather than wait for it to arrive. Once again, Mabel found herself isolated, sitting on her end of the log in the breezy sun with her scarf over her head, arms hugging herself beneath and the ends tucked into her waistband while her companions stood in the fly-infested shade.

This time they had been outfitted with broad brimmed hats draped with a screen veil that secured to a screen poncho that descended to belts at cuffs and waist. With the long heavy pants of their earlier uniform and safety boots, they now waited the drone that could be heard in the distance. Mabel sat again on the end of her log as patiently and isolated as on other days. She looked into her lap, but her eye was caught by a scrap of birch bark laying on the ground behind the log. It looked like a tag blown from the skinny tree nearby. When she looked at the trunk, she could see the light spot from which it probably was torn, and that immediately made her wonder what could have stripped it off the trunk.

When she picked up the errant scrap, her heart seemed to stop. Scratched into the light underside of the bark was her silhouette complete with a streak of red where she often wore her scarf and beside the drawing was the word "HELP?"

She looked around in bewilderment. Who could have left this? As she tipped her head down against the downdraft from the drone rotors, she made a snap decision. She scratched a 'Y' onto the bark with her fingernail and rolling to further protect herself from the hail of debris coming off the landing pad, she stuffed the bark back under the backside of the log.

Their transport drone was a four-seater remotely or autonomously controlled to take them to some destination that the training program thought needed assessing. Four huge fans lifted their passenger pod and then whizzed them across scrub that stood barely waist high with black stumps sticking through. Other patches of pointed trees stood like burrs. It was different from the forested surroundings where they lived.

"This area was burned over by a forest fire ten years ago," the instructor declared. "We have to assess the water quality of the lake and its watershed. We will be working here for at least two weeks -

depending on the reliability of our transport." It seemed that their instructor had not imagined that anything but missing transport could change that timetable. Their drone had slowed and swung around to land on a rocky outcrop beside a sandy beach. Streams splashed down the hillside on both sides of their landing site. The rotors of their drone spun to a stop.

"We'll do some practice sampling here so you know how to use the equipment," directed the Instructor. "Bring your field kits down to the beach," he said as he popped open his door to the pod. They hadn't taken two steps before they were enclosed in clouds of those small black flies that had so disrupted their program so far.

They spent the morning swiping frantically at the flies while trying to learn how to chemically test for iron, chlorides, nitrates and nitrites. They used electronic gadgets to determine carbon dioxide and oxygen levels in the water. They took water breaks and lunch huddled in the pod of their drone.

"When we bring the inflatable, we can do depth sampling out in the water," the instructor explained.

"Could we harness those flies and use them to fly this thing," asked one student with wrists that ran blood from the number of bites he had endured.

It's the harnesses that are the problem but if you can make me a million and harness the beasts," the instructor quipped, "I can train them to all fly in the same direction at once. I'd just hang you on a pole in front of the flock."

While the drone crisscrossed the lake in the afternoon taking depth measurements from a sonar dangling below it, the group did bacterial samples and then did all the tests again on the streams that entered the lake. They were getting faster by afternoon's end. Everyone was more than relieved when the drone returned to collect them for the return trip to their quarters. If things had prevented the drone from coming for them in the first place, could those same events prevent it from returning to collect them from this fly- infested torment? *Imagine having to spend the night here?* She shook the thought away and pulled her hands inside her netting.

Light rain showers drove Mabel, Harold and Irene off the balcony just about dark. Mabel had taken just about all their discussion time talking about the flies and showing them her welts. It was almost as an afterthought that she described the birchbark note. Both the others reacted with incredulity.

"What?" they asked in chorus.

Mabel had to go over every moment in detail - where everyone was, what she was doing, when she found it, and most of all what it meant.

"You wear your scarf all the time around here but nobody has material to draw you a picture. Could it have been drawn by someone in our complex, one of your classmates?" Harold asked.

"While I think you have to ask the question," Irene replied, "but the delivery and medium suggests someone out there is watching us. From this position, and it's the place we've been almost every day, we can be seen from across the lake but only with someone with a telescope. That implies this place is under outside surveillance by someone other than the people in here and they ..."

"The Sasquatch," Harold interrupted. "And the text of the note suggests they write and understand English. I wonder if there are enough of them to run a war? Could they be the reason the Accounting Files seem to have such big holes in them?"

A veil of light rain was advancing down the lake through the gloom. "Time to go in," Isabel said.

"Just how do you think they'll come to offer help?" Mabel asked as they headed for the door.

"Well, I doubt a delegation will ride up to the door to offer political asylum," Harold scoffed as he opened the door for the women.

Rain the next morning kept Mabel and her group in the lab learning to interpret their findings. As she set to her task, Mabel wondered yet again about the message on the birch bark. The secrecy of its presentation was surely confirmation of an opposing group out there. They had a picture of them. But every time they sought direct answers about the existence of such a group, their enquiries were meat with a robotic stone wall. *These sound like the bad guys*, she concluded.

The next day dawned bright and clear. They were marching along the path to the drone pad dressed in their bug suits, as they called them, with their field kits. Again, the drone was late, but not too late. They only had to sit around for a few minutes. Mabel sought her customary spot. She set her kit at the end of the log beside her and sneaked a peak behind the log.

In the place where she had left her reply two days ago was a new scrap of birch bark. The numerals "One", "Two", "Three" were written plainly on the bark by what had to be a thin-tipped pen. Over the first numeral was the word "NOW". There was a box around the third numeral. She stuffed the scrap into her boot top as the drone landed and she stooped to pick up her kit. With the others she ran across the sandy space to the pad where the drone sat, props spinning impatiently.

After dinner that night, with her scarf tied into a turban that was as bright as a landing beacon, Mabel joined her friends on the balcony. "I don't think anyone ever held evidence of first contact with an extra-terrestrial with more questions than I do with this," Harold said fingering the piece of bark. The message was still clear despite the overlay of scuffs from being in Mabel's boot before she could move it into her pocket.

"So, what happens day after tomorrow?" Irene asked.

"Well after the rain, they say we get some nice weather for a few days," Mabel offered. "Wonder if Sasquatch knows that?" She paused a moment before she added, "I'd like to visit The Storeroom tomorrow. I want to get something in George's suitcase - sort of a good-faith offering just in case I need it."

"Mind telling what?"

"George had a Swiss Army multi-tool that might be a gesture."

"Can't hurt, I guess," replied Irene. "We could go right after dinner. We'll meet you here later, Harold."

"Maybe we should skip tomorrow," Harold replied. "I don't want to draw too much attention and I think it would be better for me to go for a drink with the guys after practice."

On that note they broke up. *I wonder if he is trying to put a little space between himself and us should things go sideways,* Irene thought. *Every time we talk about that cache of luggage, he gets nervous.*

11

Day three, thought Mabel as she marched in her bug suit behind the others toward the landing pad for pickup. Today they were supposed to do water testing in the lake. A raft would be onboard for them to inflate and use. Mabel noticed the black fly population was substantially down from several days ago. She sat in her accustomed spot to await the drone. The clear sandy space surrounding the pad was dotted with rocks the size of dinner plates, she noted. That seemed strange to her. Why had she not noticed them before?

The drone approached in its usual pattern, zooming towards the 'X' mark then swerved downwind so it could swing and approach the mark upwind. She ducked her head as the prop wash passed and bent to pick up her testing kit. That's when it happened.

As she stood and turned towards the drone, she thought she saw something black drop out of the sky. She had no time to analyze what she thought she saw because the drone immediately tilted as though one corner had lost all lift. Mabel watched as the corner smashed into the dirt and a flight of broken pieces flew up from the point of impact. The three remaining turbines lifted their corners further tilting the whole machine and directing a hurricane blast sideways even as the blades sucked in the debris from the damaged one. In turn those engines immediately fragmented under the barrage of wreckage from the first blades.

The blast from the three whirling but doomed propellers blew her backwards in a cloud of dust and sand over the log she'd been sitting on into the brush behind. Clouds of dust blinded her. She rolled over to protect her face, but her arms were yanked from beneath her to drag her roughly away from the crashing sound on the landing pad.

Metal pieces were flying everywhere like food escaping from a blender. The crashing sound of splintering blades slashing through the brush behind them like a chainsaw lent wings to the feet of those hauling her. As she struggled to get her feet under her a sack was yanked over her head, and she found herself bundled into what felt like a hammock. "Don't scream," said a deep voice through the bag. "You asked for help. This is it."

The shrieks and crashes of self-destructing machinery quickly faded. She was enveloped by the thump of feet pounding on forest turf, the rhythmic puffing of heavy breathing, the background sighs of wind in the trees, the sweaty smell of heavy work and fading panic. The jolting and swaying went on for too long in her anxious state before the air turned cool. Her transport stopped. She was lowered gently to the floor and the bag pulled from her head. Against some bright background light, she could see the outlines of two tall, long-haired men dressed in dark, loose-fitting leather. Both were breathing heavily from their exertions.

"Good morning, Miss Red Scarf," one puffed as Mabel struggled to her feet. She peeled off her bug hat and felt the coolness immediately on her face. She looked around. She must be in some sort of cave.

"Good morning," Mabel replied belatedly. "My name is Mabel."

"Paul," said the first speaker holding out his hand to shake hers. His grip was firm but polite. *First contact*, Mable thought as she grasped his hand.

"Peter," said the other man shaking her hand.

Sounds Biblical to me, Mabel thought. As she dropped his hand, another man and woman came running in laughing.

"Did you see that? Now that is what I call a diversion," said the woman, through her panting. Seeing the hand of her colleague just separating she immediately offered her own. "Rachel," she said. "Zeke," said her companion.

"Mabel," she said shaking his hand. She pulled back to pull off her bug poncho. The air felt deliciously cool. She realized she was soaked in sweat. She pulled off her scarf to wipe her face.

"Did you see the way they went," Zeke was shouting as his hand arced through the air. "Rachel's was a bull's eye mine went in on the bounce." All four were slapping each other on the back and laughing. Rachel's hands flew up mimicking an explosion.

"And before the dust settled," Rachel bragged, "we got the inflatable that was thrown out of the cargo space as the cabin collapsed. It was thrown out almost on the trajectory of our rocks. The case was gouged but not punctured. How lucky was that?"

"You brought down that drone?" Mabel broke in incredulously, "How did you do that? Why did you do that?"

"We built trebuchets back in the woods. It took us a couple days to align them and get the range to the landing pad, but we could be sure that the drone would land right on the mark. It is designed to do that. We just had to time our rocks to arrive when it did."

"What's a trebuchet?"

"It's a super-sized rock-throwing sling from medieval times," Zeke bragged, as he bent his arm at the elbow and flipped the pebble in his hand forward.

Mabel shook her head at the words that seemed to come from a musty mind-corner. She was sure she had heard those words before but couldn't quite figure out what they meant, or when she had heard them. It sure wasn't in her training program.

"So," said Paul as the celebrations slid to a stop, "what did you want help with?" All eyes turned on Mabel.

She was tongue-tied. "Well, I was just curious. My friends said I should take advantage of the chance to meet you when you left that note."

"Are those the friends you meet with almost every night on the balcony?" Peter asked. "How do you know about them?"

"We've watched you for a while. Your scarf made you easy to find and follow."

"May I look at it?" asked Rachel, extending a tanned hand. Mabel handed it over noticing the woman's short nails and scratched fingers.

"Look, it changes colour as you fold it", Rachel remarked. She stepped closer to the cave entrance to admire it.

"And the other reasons are sort of complicated," Rachel continued. "My friends and I have only been relinked about a month. We wondered if there were any other people beside those in our complex. We suspected from the information we work with there might be but didn't know. If you did exist, we didn't know if you spoke English." She scanned the shadowed faces in front of her and suddenly realized that there were three of them, all male, and one of her and they stood between her and the entrance.

Rachel stepped back past them from the opening and handed her the scarf. "It is very pretty," she said.

"Would you like it?" Mabel offered on a whim. "I can get another. Look this is how I wear it…" and she quickly folded it into a strip and tied it loosely around Rachel's neck with the tail falling off her shoulder down her front.

Rachel put up a hand to ward off the garment as it came around her neck. Mabel stopped at first contact. Mabel was about to follow up on why her other reasons were complicated, but she was interrupted.

"What is relinked?" Paul asked.

Mabel was flummoxed. She wasn't sure she really knew herself. "Fifty years ago," she began, "when I was not quite fifty, I went through a process that stored all the information about every particle in me so accurately that I could be remade the way I was when I was a young woman. That was called delinking. I really didn't want to do it, but my husband tricked me into it." Even as she said it, Mabel realized that the heat that used to accompany the mere thought of that deception had gone. It was like reporting the weather - just a fact.

Rachel had lowered her hand to let Mabel finish the tying of the scarf.

"So, about a month ago," Mabel resumed, "I woke up with a new body - this one - built by a computer from the information it had stored about me and stored in a cube of gold since then. The computer re-read and recreated me over last winter. I woke up a month ago and it was half a century after I remember going to sleep. I'm really not used to being who I am. That is called relinking. All the people in the place have been through the same process." This precipitated an energetic whispered conversation amongst the men.

Mabel stepped back to admire the tied scarf; Rachel raised her chin to the others. They were too engrossed in their conversation to notice. Rachel turned to smile at Mabel. Mabel thought there was a bit of vanity in the glance as well as a social commentary on male behaviour that seemed to have transcended time.

"No, and no interest in the process of making them either," Mabel answered wryly. "That has led my friends and I to think that drugs might be added to our food without our knowing. There are other behaviours we think we notice that might be caused by chemicals in the food as well. So, when your note appeared, we thought we should try to meet you to see if you were drugged too."

"So, everybody where you live was an old person that got turned into a young person by a computer," Zeke clarified. "How old were they when they ... unlinked?"

"Right. We were all old and some might have been a hundred years or so old when they delinked. They were born - in their first life - more than a century ago from now, but we're all young now and we seem to be held in some sort of chemical suspension. Even the history we can look up does not go back to our delinking, and certainly not as far as our own memories."

"So, you don't know about the plague?" asked Paul.

"What ... plague?" Mabel asked slowly and the saying of the words made her shiver. It was suddenly cold in the cave.

"We are the children of the plague survivors," Paul said. "About the time you ... delinked, my parents came here on a rusty ship that was filled by gangsters with anyone who wanted to leave our homeland where it was too hot to live. The people survived a horrible ocean crossing and some escaped from the ship by swimming when it was not allowed to dock in the harbour. My parents were such refugees. They took a train to anywhere cool and that brought us to this area. Right behind them, like a curtain coming down, a plague was marching across the land. It seemed fuelled by the worldwide migrations that were going on to either escape the heat or find food. My parents came to work as labourers on a farm nearby and managed to survive because of their isolation and the food they could raise or find in the forest. But cities are no more - well not what they used to be. They became disease death traps, there was no, or not enough medicine to treat the ill." Saying the words sucked the breath from him.

Mabel was stunned as Paul's words drifted into a whisper.

"There are survivor groups of a couple dozen each, scattered over large distances now. We know of a few but we each fear the other because of weapons they might have or habits they have continued. I don't know of any other group that has met some group like yours."

"Harold, my friend, thinks there is a war going on somewhere between the machines or whatever that run our complexes and outside people maybe like yourselves, but he has no idea where. He says it is because the accounts he monitors don't quite balance unless there is some huge expense brought in to balance things. Whatever that expense is, it is not accessible to him. It was why he urged me to follow your note. Lastly, we were told the country was under martial law."

Rachel had wandered to the entrance to admire the ability of the scarf to change colour as she twisted it. Paul was forceful in his response. "Well, they may be at war with us, but we're too busy surviving around here." He turned toward Rachel in the entrance. "You sure you didn't come to give the natives beads," he accused.

Mabel was stunned by the charge. "I came through a hail of missiles that should have killed me and all of you as well to say hello and you have the audacity to ask me that. I find that insulting. If that is the news you want me to take back, we sadly overestimated your intentions, as you seem to have underestimated ours!" She was leaning forward and shouting in his face.

Paul raised his hand to strike her. Peter caught and held it.

"Sorry," Paul replied after a few tense seconds.

"We need to get you back," Zeke said. "You will be missed. We don't want to encourage a widespread search."

They decided they could meet again if Mabel was seen on the balcony by the lake wearing her new scarf with the knot on her right shoulder and the end hanging down that side. They'd leave a note as before. They offered her all the food supplies they had with them if Mabel and her friends wanted to eat items, they would know were not treated with whatever chemicals they feared were in the food. To make room in her pockets for the leaf-wrapped bundles, she removed the Swiss Army knife and handed it to Zeke in exchange. It caused another discussion among the men that seemed to go on for a while. Mabel had retreated to the mouth of the cave where she and Rachel were experimenting with different ways to use the scarf and discussing the food packets.

"Thank-you," Zeke said, holding up the clasped tool. "This has tips that will allow us to work on things we had found but couldn't open." She recovered her bug suit and was bundled back into the hammock in which she had been carried away from the drone landing pad.

Rachel handed the hood to put on herself. "So you can't find us," she explained. "They'll let you off near the landing site. Tell them you ran away and got lost."

It might have been twenty minutes later that she was set down and told to close her eyes. Hands helped her to her feet, and she did as instructed. Her hood was pulled away and she was pushed off balance. She flailed her arms to keep from falling. When she turned to see which one had pushed her, nobody was there - nor was the hood or hammock.

"Which way ..." she said to the forest about her. In the distance she heard activity that sounded more and more like a branch chopper shredding brush as she walked in the direction she had been pushed.

12

"My clothes were declared disposable with the tears and picks," Mabel explained on the deck after supper. She was wearing her new scarf tied into a turban and a new copy of her pants and stretchy black top she'd been 'born into' when she delinked. "Do you know that the last pieces of that whole wreckage - all the pieces of the blades and body - went into that chopper before the end of the day? I didn't see any big motor parts when I got back. I stood beside the landing pad for ten minutes before anyone noticed me. When I asked where the instructor and my classmates were, the guy in charge of the cleanup didn't know. How they could have survived if they didn't duck and run..." Her words petered out. "The things coming out of that wreck slashed down the bush like a mower for farther than this balcony is long. I told the supervisor in charge of the robot cleaners that I ran for my life and got lost."

"Sounds like an edited copy," Irene replied.

"It is," Mabel whispered. "I met them," Mabel continued.

The others leaned closer.

"Three men and a woman. They hauled me out of the line of fire and then bundled me up so I couldn't see them till we were pretty far away. They've been watching us since I got my scarf. They call me the lady with the red scarf. I left my old scarf with the woman. Rachel is her name."

"Were there only four?" Harold asked.

"That's all I met but they put a bag over my head so I couldn't see where we went. It was not too far away, and it was in some sort of cave. I got the feeling there might be more not too far away. They said they were the survivors of some sort of Plague that swept the world ..."

"Did you say plague - like Black Death?" Irene gasped.

"At least that bad - probably worse. There are no cities anymore."

"What?" came the stunned response.
"The contagion got started and was carried as people migrated in national numbers from places where it was too hot to live or grow food. That confirms what you figured, Harold. The tropics are too hot for normal living." They considered her words while Mabel figured out what to tell next.

"They also said there are other small groups, but they are reluctant to communicate with them because they're not sure how aggressive or how well armed they might be. So once again, it seems to confirm your supposition, Harold."

"Was it just a co-incidence that the drone crashed on the day you were to meet therm. That's what the news is on the screens and at meal hour," Harold asked.

"They brought it down," Mabel whispered, "with rocks and something called a trebu … something. They knew about them from medieval times."

"Are you sure?" gasped Irene. "They intentionally shot down a drone?"

"They didn't shoot it down with a gun. This trebu-thing tosses rocks up in the air and they just timed them to come down on the drone as it landed. They knew exactly where the drone would land. They said their rocks smashed the blades of one of the rotors and the whole thing went unbalanced and smashed itself after that."

"That suggests they have access to history that we can't find on our computers. The excuse online is that it was never converted over from binary days. It thickens the theory that there is a conspiracy to rewrite, or un-write history."

"And they are astounded that we are alive from a Pre-Plague era. There is nobody in their world as old as we are - or look as good either," she laughed.

"Oh, and they said that if we were worried about our food being contaminated, they gave me some of their food to eat instead of what is served here. It is like a nutribar I think. I have them in my book bag. They are hard and really chewy. They taste strange - like really tart - and there is probably lots of fat in them because of their slippery-ness. I don't know if I should tell you what the protein source is though."

Harold groaned. "Please don't say it's bugs or worms."

"How did you know?" Mabel looked at him in surprise.

"It was a frat party thing back in my earlier life. They were chocolate-coated grasshoppers or crickets I think."

"Well, that is what Rachel said these are but without the chocolate. She said the flavouring was cranberries and they grow wild around here."

"What's left to report?" Mabel asked herself. "Paul likely has issues with women being as smart or able as he is and maybe an anger management issue. Zeke really liked the knife and said it would help them get into things they found instead of smashing them. That suggests they are rather busy scavengers." Her companions were silently looking out over the railing at the lake. "Oh, last item. If I knot my scarf on the right and let the ends hang down my right side, they will take it as a signal that we want to meet them, and they'll leave a note of when they can do it in the same place. They seem to be watching us all the time."

"Holy smoke," groaned Harold. "I just found out I'm Methuselah to a bunch of youngsters, I missed a world-wide pandemic, and I can have bugs instead of drugged food for breakfast, lunch and supper. God I'm glad I got up this morning! Not sure if I can take getting up tomorrow though. Good night."

*

"Those nutribars from Paul and company might be what the Hebrews subsisted on while crossing the desert. They're in two layers - like entree and dessert," Harold reported three days later when they gathered at their favourite spot. "You can peel the backing off like cardboard and chew it forever. I think it must be some sort of meat jerky. The softer stuff might be like a stale donut, deep-fried and tart. I take a bite of it and wash it down quickly, then chew on the backing underneath for an hour. I must confess I'm beginning to feel like myself rather than the zombie that was walking around in my skin. What did you think," he asked Mabel and Irene. They had agreed that Harold should be the guinea pig while they would be the taste testers in the focus group.

"In my earlier life I could never imagine putting something like that in my mouth, Maybe delinking disconnected me from my cultured palette of days past," Mabel said, "but I did, and I agree about the jerky. It will never be a favourite but it is satisfying, even though it as tough as a boot."

"You know," she added as an afterthought, "this makes three things I've noticed about myself since relinking. I used to be obsessive about wardrobe. I'm not now. I used to be really bitchy about what I ate - sent stuff back at a restaurant for no reason - did the tantrum thing. And I'd have gone ballistic over fly bites like a few weeks ago. Maybe there is Valium or its cousin in the food. Anyway, what is your learned assessment, Irene?"

"Well, I was never a fan of donuts, or anything deep-fried but I have to admit, the bite I had, I could swallow. I used to be a closet gum-chewer. I could never chew it at the office - bad example you know and off-putting to the other execs, so I liked being able to tuck a chunk of that stuff in my cheek and gnaw on it all day. I pitched my dinner and never missed it. And I will agree with you Harold, I really feel sharper, the less I eat at the food court. Speaking of which," she turned abruptly away to look over the lake and lowered her voice.

"We had a third type of droid appear in the shop for maintenance. You know about the drinkbots and the Cameronbots. This looks like a Cambot - same frame, bigger wheels, more clearance but has no screen in its chest. I think they do maintenance in the service tunnels."

"Now you mention it, that was the kind of droid cleaning up the drone crash. I don't think they had screens on their chests either," Mabel added.

"So, what I did was copy the droid's IDs as part of its maintenance and I used it to access the lock on the outside door. It worked. We can now get out of jail. And don't dance like that Mabel, you'll attract the camera's attention."

"I wonder if we should call out for pizza?" Mabel asked.

"Sure, let's try," Irene agreed.

"Sounds like party game time," Mabel suggested, taking off her red scarf with a flourish and shaking her hair into the wind. With a flourish, she tied it on the right side and let the ends fall across her right chest. "Now if I looked in here for lunch, do you think they might get the idea that we're looking for a food delivery? She boosted her book bag to the railing and made a production out of searching its depths. She slid it over to Irene to do the same. Irene returned it with a sad shrug.

"You too, Harold." He searched and pretended to find a crumb.

"Was that a flash of red I saw on the cliff over there?" Irene asked.

"Didn't see." the other's replied.

*

Harold and Mabel were hurrying down the path towards the landing pad as soon as they could gracefully get out of work and meet. The outer door clicked open when Harold held up the code that identified them as a droid. They counted on Irene, still working late, to be able to cancel any alert that might appear on screen that the door had been opened. Mabel said it would take them ten minutes to get to the log where a message would be dropped. The pad was within sight when Harold spotted the metal bar stuck into the tree like a spear.

"This must be part of the drone that the droids didn't collect," he said as he tried to wiggle it loose.

"They were programmed to pick up what was on the ground, and this is above their reach even if they did notice it."

"Did we just bend it?" she asked as her feet touched the ground.

"I think it is still straight," he said but didn't back up. leaving her pinned against the tree by his weight as he looked on one side then the other. He backed up. "I need a rock to bang it back up."

"I'll go see if we have a message?" Mabel said fas she dropped to the ground. "You work on this." She hurried down the path leaving Harold ramming at the metal with a branch. Instead of a scrap of birch bark, she found a a pile of food packets She could only carry six because they kept slipping out of her cupped hands. She got back to Harold and was headed for the door when he asked for her help again. They did the hoist and pull down. This time the bar wiggled down more easily.

"I'll get the rest." Mabel ran back to the log. She looked around to see if Paul or any of his group might be there. Nobody. She laid on the log one of her gold coins that she had snipped out of her suitcase when she got the Swiss Army Knife. A chipmunk dashing from the pile of packets squeaked in alarm. So did she. Having looked carefully for another interloper and found none, she scooped the remaining packets into her arms and stepped quickly back up the path.

"Hurry, Harold, we're way over time," she puffed as she passed. "Bring those ones."

Harold was pulling and pushing the bar easily now and it slipped slightly free with each pass. With a grunt it came loose. "Coming," he called to Mabel. He tucked the bar under his arm, scooped up the food and hustled after her. Mabel placed the food packets into the bottom of her book bag that she had left holding the door ajar. With her foot now holding the door, she extended the bag to Harold who unceremoniously dumped his packets on top of hers, pulled the door wide and they both stepped inside, puffing. The door clicked behind them.

"What took so long?" hissed Irene when they all re-gathered at the balcony railing after meeting in the library. They each felt they could talk more freely and could hide hand movements from cameras that lined the space when they were in the open air. The reason for meeting in the library was to get book bags to hold the collection of big books each had checked out. On the balcony, Irene surreptitiously slid them each four food packets to bury below their books. To any observer behind them, they seemed engrossed in a study of the stars using big sky atlases as the pinpoints emerged in the twilit sky.

"Harold spotted a piece of metal stuck in a tree over head-height that the droids missed."

"It's a rod about my thumb-size in diameter," Harold interrupted, "and it is twisted into a point on the end that was stuck in the tree. The other end is sort of curved like a wrecking bar. It just looked too useful to leave there, but it took some doing to work it loose. Man, that hit the tree at speed. Anyway, it fits into my book bag quite nicely. It makes me feel like a second-story man."

"Well, I was glad I stayed in the shop," Irene explained. "Every five minutes, the door alert flashed up on the screen. You'd have had company if I hadn't cancelled each message with an error override. It's also interesting to me that the door monitor registered it as "Open" if it was. When it's closed the light goes out. It doesn't say "Locked." So as long as the door is closed, the machine thinks it's locked. All you need to do is put a stick in the latch to jam it and you can come back and open the door any time you need."

"You know Harold and I have said that even though we've been chewing on other food for only a couple days, we both feel sharper, like we can figure out things and have the motivation to do so. That was pretty sharp of you to catch that repeat message that the door was open," Mabel complimented.

"It's as though a fog or some sort of low-level headache is fading," Irene agreed. "Anyway, it looks like we have supplies for a week. We sure should know if this is going to work by then."

By the way, while you two were gallivanting about the countryside, I decided that the droid whose identity I copied needed a repair to the tool-drive assembly. There is a tray of sockets in it that each fit on a hexagonal drive in its arm. I replaced the relevant parts, so we have a set of sockets and the hex stub they fit on. I'm working on finding a vice grip to grab the stub so we can turn things."

"You are feeling better," Mabel said. "Age and deception seem about to overcome youth and skill."

*

Irene met them on the deck two nights later with relief written all over her face. "I found there is a check system that weighs the weight of scrap pieces we remove from droids," Irene revealed as they each got out their sky maps. "It doesn't do it by machine but by the week. It is so that the recycle system can be balanced with new production needs, I guess. "Anyway," she continued, "I caught it in time to add chips from the drone crash to the box that had missing tool sockets etc. That was close. We only dump our recycle parts each week. The machine doesn't analyze the things in the box. Only the mass of the box is compared against the mass of the parts that have been replaced. Makes sense - all the next step needs to know is how much material it has to work with. That determines how much energy is needed to melt the charge. So, it looks like we can continue to fly under the radar. I also picked up a pail of crash scraps just for future use. I can always say it got pushed out of the way and missed.

"And I also did some more scouting. We were right. There is a whole system of pipes, nicely painted pale blue, that drizzles something onto food as it passes to the conveyor that directs food to the different restaurants in the food court. I think the blue machines add the additive we had suspected are drugging everyone. You can tell it isn't spices - you can smell the spigots that do that. This is odourless, is linked to a bunch of different containers, as you'd expect if different people were being catered to, and it is added to every dish that comes out."

"Well, it's too cloudy for star gazing," Mabel observed. "Maybe we should check it out? Harold?"

"Agreed."

When Irene showed them the equipment, they agreed. The rank of four sealed blue bottles with lengthy number codes was what they expected. The best fix, if they wanted to turn off the supply, would be the plastic tubing that Mabel remembered was in George's suitcase. It was the link between his oxygen tank and facemask and was long enough for him to move around the room without moving the tank much. "If it won't fit, we could warm the tubing by sticking it in the micro-waved drinks as they come out. That should let us jam it over the fitting but where do we drain it to?"

"Well, there seems to be a drip catcher that goes into a drain below the tray conveyor," Irene observed, bending and peering into the machinery. She struggled to get around the equipment. "Yep," she called, "I can see it. Now help me out."

"So, we could do this, but the question is whether we should?" Irene said as they returned down the tunnel. "I mean we're making decisions for a lot of others if we decide to turn off the glow machine, but I used to do that all the time in my other life."

"Corporately, we'd decide around a table, and after a lot of minions gathered research, that it was beneficial to the corporation to move a production line. We'd offer severance packages to those who wouldn't move, and transportation help to those who would but I didn't have to arrange for new schools for kids or nursing care for a parent. My salary kept coming and I could count on a bigger bonus when the move happened. There was no downside for me. I sort of see that differently now. What if people go into depression or go suicidal when the sedatives stop? What if we unleash some sort of sociopath or dictator?"

"What if there is some medication, in the cocktail, that is keeping us all healthy, like a vaccine or something" Irene continued. "We can stay healthy because we're the only ones off the grid. It's a bit like measles - do you remember that? Everyone got immunized - well except for a few - but even they didn't get exposed because of the herd resistance."

"If there is something specialized coming out of a spigot back there," Harold suggested as though he hadn't heard Irene's concern, "your own cocktail of stuff, I wonder if there isn't some sort of generalized brew added to the water, like flouride but designed to soften your thoughts rather than harden enamel?" he asked.

"Didn't you hear what I said?"

"Yes," Harold apologized, "I just couldn't get off the track my mind was on. It is a habit of forensic auditing from my past. Just because you find one thing wrong doesn't mean there aren't many other transgressions, even bigger ones, that are more deeply hidden. Sometimes the ones you find easily were the sacrificial lambs. Geez, do you suppose the air might be flavoured as well?"

"What a bunch of killjoys you guys are," Mabel chimed in critically. "Here I was getting all excited about saving our little world, turning them back into the nice people they used to be, and you turned the job into some philosophical conspiracy contest."

"I think you have to accept the fact that just because all those people had enough money to jump the mortality cue," Irene replied with a bit of an edge to her voice, "they weren't thinking of anyone's good but their own. Don't give them credit for being nice to anyone but themselves. And secondly, if we remove the medical gauze they are wrapped in now, we might find some rather ugly truths below. Things might be more complicated than we thought."

"Right," Harold agreed.

They returned in silence to the library where they had left their book bags, then went out onto the deck. Twilight had all but gone. Patches of clouds hid some of the sky. They got out their books as though they were continuing the star studies.

"Well, I've got only a couple days of supplies left," Harold observed. "If we aren't going to turn off the medicals by then, we need a Plan B. The default plan is to go back to LaLa land with the others."

"Well, we could run off to join Peter and Paul," Mabel suggested.

"Life sentence at hard labour is what I'd guess that is," Harold shot back.

"I think we should start talking to people," Irene suggested. Let's try to find out who did what in a past life, ask about how they feel about things now. Maybe there is an intermediate step - we bring a few into our circle first?"

"Sounds rather Olympian, eh?" suggested Harold. "I have a growing feeling of deity as we decide if we should welcome more mortals to our realm. But let's not give them fire," Harold commented sarcastically.

"You worked alone too long," Irene commented.

The next night, it was raining. They sat alone in the top row of the Amphitheatre watching the rain pour down on the deck beyond the doors.

"I've been mining the computer for nuggets," Harold reported. "Under the guise of asset assessment. Do you remember when we came from the elevator when we first came to this level. We got off the elevator and turned left, through those fire-doors over there," he hooked his thumb over his shoulder, "into here? Well, if you go right from the elevators, there is the section of the building we entered when we came to delink. There is a set of fire-doors there as well to separate it off. Well, I found that whole wing - tower actually - is mothballed. It's got no heat, no light, no power. That means there are no more people coming into the system. You'd have to ask why. The reason might be the Plague our friends outside mentioned. Anyway, those you see and those in storage are all there are - well here. I don't know how many other sites there are. I have no idea where our predecessors went."

"How many others are in storage, Harold?" Irene asked.

I can't tell from what I can access at this stage. Based on the space I'd guess the facility relinks maybe a hundred in a year, max, how many classmates have we total?"

"Seventy-six," Irene said. "I counted them in the food lineup.

"Anyway," Harold added. "There is a whole tower not in use."

"I've been exploring the service tunnels," Irene added. "You were right about the water, Harold. I found the same blue-coloured tank - only bigger - attached to the pipe coming from the filtering process. It's a really bright light they use to treat the water, maybe like Ultra-violet - it isn't chemical - but right after this dazzling bunch of tubes, there was our friendly blue bottle with two other tanks marked "Chlorine" and "Fluorine". The Chlorine may be a back-up or old tech. It seems turned off. Maybe it's corroded closed. No smell either. But the blue tank can be turned off with a single quarter-turn toggle. I tried it and it moves easily. I also found that I can take off the handle on the valve with one of the droid drivers I rescued, I can move the handle to appear that valve is closed even if it appears open - or ..."

"Open when it really is closed," Harold completed. "How would a droid deal with that paradox Irene? If it came to replace the tank and its first step was to close the valve. it would actually open it. Then when it disconnected the pipe, water or tank contents would spurt all over the place. Then what?"

"I'd guess it would fry the electronics. But it would only try to do that if a sensor said the tank needed replacing. To do that, it would have to get a signal that it was "Empty." I've seen that control board and it only gives one condition. In this case "Empty." If that light is not on, it seems to be presumed, by the droids, that the tank is full enough not to need replacement. and they ignore it. It's like the outside door, If the "Open" light is off, it is presumed to be closed - and locked."

"So, turning off the tank, should forever seem to keep the tank full even though the toggle looks like it is turned on."

"That's my guess unless there is some other protocol based on inventory or past usage rate. Even so, it the droid got a command to replace it, and then turned the toggle, it would get shorted out. Would it figure out that something was wrong?"

"My guess is no. I don't think it was programmed to solve problems only to follow the plan. If the water didn't fry it, the paradox might."

"My last offering tonight is about the air system; I have no idea if or where there are aromatics in the ventilating system. My guess is that it would not require a ladder to change out anything that might be part of the universal sedative plan but where that is - I just haven't figured out yet."

"I've talked to a few. I'm trying not to make it obvious," Mabel said. "I've come across some major executives and some medical specialists, but they are monumentally indifferent. I mean all the drive and questioning the analysis they'd have done every day ... it isn't there at all. I mean I feel sort of ambivalent about a lot of things, but these people are like ... who cares?"

They all sat looking out the window, listening to the patter of the rain.

"Trying to bring anyone else into the loop right now is procrastinating," Irene concluded. "I think we should go ahead with what we've got. I run out of food tomorrow," Irene said.

"I've already run out," Harold interjected.

Mabel dug about in her bag and found a couple food lumps. She held them out to Harold who put up his hands in token protest but took them before she put them back. During the wordless exchange she tried to remember the last time she ever shared stuff in her other life. Nothing came back. *Will I be like that again?* she wondered.

"When?" she asked.

"How about now?"

"They sat a moment looking down at their hands. Harold licked his sticky fingers. Irene slapped the table. "OK. Let's do it." They got up and did.

*

"Something is happening, just listen to the sound of conversation," Irene noted three days later as they walked through the food court.

"Right," agreed Mabel. "It sounds like a high school hallway at break time. I watched one couple in tears, hugging each other. They've been relinked for over a month, and this is the first time I've seen that sort of emotion. They walk everywhere hand in hand. I thought I heard them talking about farming and wanting to leave soon to go back to where they came from."

"I met a guy who used to be a mechanical engineer,". Harold added. "We went exploring in the service tunnels. He found the central air conditioning on a map and sure enough there is a big tank coloured light blue attached to the air supply. He said it was like a giant air freshener or humidifier and it has all sorts of risks for culturing bacteria. He said they tore out a lot of them after they were linked to something called Legionnaire's disease. Do you ever hear about that?"

"Nope."

"Not me."

"Anyway, he's full of questions about how the place works and who's in charge and how mundane the training courses are. He thought they'd be more challenging. So far, he said, he hadn't learned anything he didn't already know, it is just that it didn't matter a toot to him before - now it does. He's ready to go out and start building more office towers again. And he sounds rather nettled that that we haven't seen Brian lately. Is that the guy who was on stage that first day we came up here? I hadn't even noticed." He stopped before he brought out his big concern.

"I think we should call a meeting - just like there was that first day here - only we call it to clue people in to the fact that there have been a few changes."

"Who do we ask to get permission to use the hall? asked Mabel.

"Let's ask Brian next time we see him," Irene suggested wryly, "and if we don't see him before, maybe we ask forgiveness later."

"I've been wondering how overt we should be about doing that," Harold added. "I think we need to spread the word because this is going to be about as dramatic as coming up here in the first place. Remember how everyone stood around in little groups. It was like preschoolers in the park. Then people started to socialize - well they talked to each other - but the content was pretty banal and that was likely because of the drugs in the food. People are coming out of their haze now. The hearing protection is coming off, figuratively speaking. I agree it's a good idea to give everyone a heads-up but to do so might draw fire from whoever put all those controls in place. Do you think we should be a little careful?"

"I've been hunting the sensor system - the ones the droids service," Irene said. "There are cameras all over the place - watching. If we wanted to have a meeting without alerting the off-site watchers, if there are any, we'd have to do something about the cameras. Shutting them down would set off alarms, but substituting a loop of pre-recorded visuals wouldn't set off any bells - I don't think. I'd have to figure out how to do that. Maybe one of our group has more skill than I at doing this."

"I know a woman who made her millions in the gaming industry, maybe she could offer some insight," suggested Mabel.

"Can you get her to meet me?" Irene asked.

"I can ask."

"OK, let's shoot for two more days - not tomorrow but after dinner on the night following - in the Amphitheatre."

*

"Good evening. Good evening" she called more loudly. When the crowd quieted, she continued. She was not on the stage but speaking from the side aisle at the front. "My name is Irene. I've spoken to some of you in the last week or so. Since relinking, a couple friends and I have found out something we thought you all should know. We believe we have found that we are all being drugged." She pushed past the gasps and the incredulity. "Chemicals are being added to our food and water and air to make us lethargic, indifferent and dumbing us down. We thought you should know." A rattle of voices broke out forcing her to stop. Out of the noise one theme arose.

"How do you know? Prove it?"

Irene held up her hand and the shouting stopped to let her answer.

"I can give you details but showing you all might not be wise considering that someone installed the stuff. If they find out, you might be the target of a tough response. But we could take a small group to show what we found. Suffice it to say, three days ago we turned off the chemicals - executive decision on our part. So, our proof is what changes if any, you might have experienced over that time. Do you feel more aware now than a week ago? Do you feel more alert? Are you less tolerant of the movie schedule?" There was a stunned silence. Before people started to share any awareness of changes they might have experienced over the week, Irene pushed on.

"We sought to protect you all during this meeting. We didn't count on it going on for long. The cameras in this place and the places you should be at present, have been disabled but in a few minutes, they will go back into service, and we should look like we're going about things normally. At present, the food supply is drug free. The water is clean and has fluoride in it to give you strong enamel to reduce dental decay but nothing else. We're working on the air. As time goes on, we ask you to monitor yourselves and trade what you notice quietly. We'd like to gather next week, same time. Can we ask you to disperse before our time runs out on the camera coverage? Stop us at any time to chat about what we said. We hold star study classes on the deck each evening after dark." Irene stopped and led her team, all with their book bags, up the aisle to the top and right out onto the deck. She ignored the whispered exchanges that questioned her sanity perhaps paranoia. They were besieged by new stargazers on the deck that night.

*

"I don't know who you are young lady, but I think you must be right about the food," said a tall man with a no-nonsense manner. "My time before this week was like days with the flu at work back in my old life. It is really only today that I've started to feel like my old self. Good Job! When can we expect you to fix the air problem?"

Irene jerked back in surprise. The silence stretched.

"Well?" persisted her interrogator, aggressively.

Irene ground her teeth a moment and pinned him with her eyes. "Sir, I dealt with a lot of people like you in my corporate world before. You may be surprised to find how many others here are like you. If we find the air is doctored and where, I'll expect you to report with the right wrench to share in the work. Maybe a drink would be appropriate for now," and she flashed him a humourless smile.

The man was clearly surprised at a less than subservient response. He backed up and stumbled to reply. He looked down as though he accepted that he was out of line, but he was still on autopilot. "Keep me informed," he added quietly and then added … "please" and turned away.

"This whole place is full of alpha males or their surrogates," Harold offered, as he leaned over after Irene had a moment to cool off. "Nobody but his type had the money to get in."

"So, I guess we'll find out who the team builders really are and who the management failures were then and are now. You know this problem seemed so simple a week ago when we put that tube over the spigot that squirted the meds on the food. Do you suppose we have to reinstate that stuff - maybe a split mealtime - some with some without just for social harmony?"

"I really want to thank you for your action," said the young lady who interrupted as she joined them at the railing. "You are absolutely right. My husband and I are actually getting to know each other again." She nudged Irene and gave her a knowing wink. "Nights are now worth waking up for. This is better than our honeymoon." After a satisfying chuckle she asked, "Do you think we can arrange for transport any time soon? We'd like to go back to Toronto to work. John is anxious to see how the hospital that carries our name is doing, He was so proud to endow it."

Mabel was about to blurt out a response when Harold nudged her and stepped in. "I guess that is further down our list of priorities. We'd focused on the food and water, and we really didn't know what the effects would be. As Irene said, we think we should check out the air supply with someone who knows better than we do, and someone, a former engineer and developer, has already stepped up to help. Maybe you can bring up that topic at the next meeting? I didn't catch your name?" They traded names and then she saw her husband through the crowd.

"There's John now." she said pointing to the man smiling across the room. I think I'm getting a signal." She gave Irene and Mabel a wink. "Goodnight."

"Thanks," Mabel said to Harold as they turned back to look over the lake. "I forgot that they don't know yet. You know maybe turning off the meds wasn't such a good idea."

"Done now," said Harold grimly. "But she brings up a really interesting point. Where is the transport chain that supplies this place? And the power supply - where does that come from? If there are no more people coming in, and that seems to be the case based on the closure of that wing, it was part of the deal that we could travel when we relinked. There should still be regular connections to the airport."

"Did you say travel?" said one of a pair of women who had joined them. "I didn't mean to intrude but I couldn't help overhearing you talking about travel options. We expect to travel also. When we asked to make arrangements, they told us in the travel office that we had to nail down our destinations a little more clearly. To help they offered virtual reality tours of their facilities. They really are wonderful. You put on a hood with a screen inside and you are there. You can actually feel the breeze in your face as you look around. You smell the flowers - it is really incredible," she gushed. "We put in our request for Venice. They said that the request is being processed as we speak. It first had to go to Scheduling. We're pretty excited about going there soon."

"I'm really anxious to hear about your arrangements and how long they take to process," Harold replied. "Could you let me know when you have a time?"

"Sure," she said. I'm Gloria and this is my friend Krista. We put in our request earlier today. They said it would only take a day or so to get a reply."

Irene and Mabel turned away from Harold and the women who were making arrangements to meet. "God. What have we done?" she whispered into the darkness.

*

Irene called the meeting to order as scheduled. The room noise was much more animated than before. Obviously, something had changed. She expected to announce that tonight.

In preparation, the ladies had told her that their plans to visit Venice were not approved yet because of the high demand for accommodation there. Harold had found that beachfront property belonging to DL Inc. in Florida and Indonesia had been written off. Whether it had been earthquake or weather-related in Indonesia was not clear. Harold guessed that the seawater might be up to the second floor and the foundations threatened if the global warming that had been underway when he delinked had proceeded as scientists expected. If they were gone, Venice, which he said was six inches from oblivion, would likely also be gone. There was supposed to be some sort of barrier to protect the city. Right! Any delay in booking a visit was likely a ploy to disguise the fact that it was gone.

"Again, we have only disguised our presence from the cameras for a short time," Irene began. "I'm pleased to announce that we found and disconnected the chemical doctoring of the air supply. Our air, water and meals are now medicine-free." Warm applause greeted the pronouncement.

"My other news will take a lot of getting used to." The buzz settled into silence. "Climate changes predicted by scientists when we delinked have happened and continue. Sea levels have risen and will rise even more. Those of you planning to travel will find any seaside destinations will not be available. They have likely been sunk!" Righteous rage rose from the seats. Irene had to shout over the tumult. "We cannot prove this yet, but we do know of several seaside sites that used to be available have been written off the books. They weren't sold off they simply were noted as losses – the whole value of those properties. Not even the land lot value was retained."

"There is more," she said, and the voices subsided. "There is more you need to know." The angry comments faded to silence.

"While we were delinked, there were massive migrations for social and economic reasons. Places on the Earth got too hot to grow food or even live. Waves washed away whole nations. At the same time as these tumultuous times, a pandemic struck, the like of which has not been seen since the Black Death in Medieval times. There was not enough time to create the vaccines; the migrations spread the disease too fast. Only our isolation saved this establishment." The room was deathly quiet.

"The result has been world-wide depopulation," Irene continued quietly. "We believe we are one of only a few communities left in this area. We've met a few survivors outside this place. They are nomadic scavengers. They are all young. As we cannot believe their youth and calamity, they cannot believe our age and affluence. There is some evidence from our financial studies that DL Inc. is fighting a war somewhere, but we have only circumstantial evidence of that. What we are sure of is that we are a colony in a devastated world. The supplies that appear robotically to sustain us might continue or cease at any time.

Outraged cries rose from the room. Irene held up her hand. Others shouted down their companions to let her continue.

"You were relinked according to the contract you made with DL Inc. You might not have agreed to the sedated situation into which you returned. Maybe it was in the fine print. We, as neighbours, found that condition and awakened you to the world that now exists. It was an executive decision on our part. Many of you will understand that decision because you made it on behalf of many others in your earlier life." A rumble of grudging acknowledgement confirmed her action.

"The decisions that are before us now probably include a return to that chemical state, or doing something in the world we live in." She scanned the room of angry and frustrated faces and hurried on. "With time running out on our concealment from the cameras, we should again return to where we should be and continue our conversations in small groups. I would ask you all to be calm as you leave - please. I know it is a shock, but there was no other simple way to tell you of your situation." There was a scary timbre to the grumblings she heard before she reached to door.

"What happened to my lab?" asked one voice in anguish.

13

"Roger," said Harold's new companion by way of introduction. "Roger the Dodger" to my few friends and many enemies alike. I have not opted for retraining yet. In fact, I used to lay awake at night wondering why I was so happy with watching old movies. I never did that in my earlier life. But I just could not work up the energy to give a damn – well until this week. My old curiosity is back. So where do you access the computer network from?

"Well maybe you could sign up for 'Asset management' training and we could at least work in the same space, suggested Harold. "You'd likely have your own workstation. If you don't mind me asking, how did you earn your nickname?"

"Well, I dodged everything in a computer. I could make more money hacking than working, and it was much more fun. When I retired, they called me by my middle name."

"Which was…?"

"Brooklyn. I was worth a whole team."

"But the Dodgers played for Los Angeles."

"Not originally – and my middle name wasn't Spanish."

"I presume you can sign up, on your room terminal, for retraining and meet me in the classroom tomorrow," Harold smiled.

"As you wish."

Mabel, shouldered aside by Harold's new friend, whispered into Irene's ear. "I'd really like to visit the trunk room. Could we do that right now – or as soon as you can escape?"

Irene made eye contact and squeezed her hand.

"You're saying that those left out there," pointing across the lake, "are a bunch of scroungers?" said a man approaching them.

"I've met a small group and I would not call them scroungers," Mabel said with an edge to her voice. "That word used to have such a demeaning overtone. Those people helped my friends and I by giving us uncontaminated food that sustained us long enough and got us clean enough to see through the chemical fog. I'd call them big-time helpers. Because of them, you can ask that question."

The man stepped back – hands held up in front of him. "I didn't realize I'd come on so strong," he placated. "I'm just running on autopilot, I guess. But you know something?" His face was crinkled in puzzlement. "Just now, as you spoke, I felt I was watching a movie of myself standing on this balcony. Like I was out of this body. If you had talked to me that way back then," his thumb flipped over his shoulder towards a distant time, "I'd have blown sky-high. Now it's as though I have this schizophrenic being inside that just hammered my old me, flat. Maybe it's a left-over effect. I sort of want to tell you to shut up and do the job I expect you to do, but at the same time, I talking to you telling you things I'd never have told anyone before."

"Well, that's about the dumbest come-on line, I've heard," Irene interjected.

The man looked puzzled – maybe contrite. His mouth worked but he didn't seem to be able to frame a come-back.

"To back up my friend," Irene added. "She did have contact with a few who seemed like they would be really resourceful friends to have. But they decide if they want to contact us if we call. It's a bit like leaving a message. Did you ever need to get in touch with someone? You left messages all over the place, but they didn't call back. It's like that. We wait to see if they respond to any message we leave. Does that make it clear enough who is in the driver's seat – to coin an old expression?"

"As crystal," said the man. "By the way, that's something else I can't recall seeing around here – crystal wine glasses. Have you?"

"Probably part of a safety protocol," Irene offered. "Can't cut much with a plastic tumbler, nor does it break if you throw it into the fireplace. Come to think of it, I haven't found a fireplace except for the one on the video screen."
The man left shaking his head.

By bedtime, a committee had formed among those who had gathered on the balcony to study the stars that night.

As they finally broke free of the crowd, Mabel said, "You know that guy behaved just like the other one the first night. I noticed confusion in myself when I looked at my wardrobe and found it would fit in an envelope. Is it possible that the computer experience – delinking and relinking – has had some sort of effect that grinds off abrasive personality – I mean beside the chemical thing?"

Irene didn't reply to that question but asked one of her own. "Why do you need to get in the luggage room?"

"There is something I want to get from my suitcase." They walked in silence with the unspoken identity question hanging. It's a keepsake – no it is something that was really special to me at one time, and I want to find out if it still is, by getting it."

"Hmmm."

"Do you think we should tell everyone about the trunk room?"

"Not if we want to keep it and everything else a secret."

"Is there a case to make for the contents of the trunk room being a finder's keepers thing?"

Irene did not reply. When they arrived at the door, she said, "Give me a boost up."

In a moment Irene was through the ceiling tile and opening the door inside. "Be quick," she said. "I'll wait here."

Mabel tore loose the quilted container of gold coins, tucked the upper edge under the lower binding of her bra and the bottom quilt hem under her waistband then pulled down the bottom of her T. The diamonds went into her breast cups on each side. On a whim, she rattled some of the drawers in the case and then picked out a compact. She closed everything up and hurried back to the door holding the case. She made a show of tucking it into her shirt down her neckline. "I used to spend a lot of time with this," she said.

Irene was tucking another travel journal and pencil into her waistband.

She looked at Mabel's item and then her face with arched eyebrows.

Mabel ignored the incredulous glance and stepped into the hall. The door clicked behind her as she side-stepped to be in place to catch Irene's feet when she dropped down from the ceiling.

*

"We found the loading docks," Irene said to the committee who met on the balcony after lunch. "Mabel suggested that if food was being brought in, garbage had to go out, so we followed up any funny smells and found the loading complex."

"Don't you just love these new bodies?" Mabel added, "I can smell things I never noticed before." She was inhaling the water scent of a hot summer afternoon.

"It's not garbage as we knew it, or groceries," Irene summarized. "Everything comes in standardized tanks on transport trunks – must be battery driven. There were no drivers in the trucks we saw back in. As soon as they did, the roof on the truck rolled back and hoists lifted the metal boxes off on their pallets and set them in place beside similar ones that were connected to pipes. I think what is inside must be feed stock for the food or clothing manufacturing systems. Once again, we saw no people - only a couple droids. One disconnected a tank and connected the new one. Then the hoist lifted out the old one and set it on the truck. The automation is amazing."

"Glad you found that," said Roger. "I only found the computer records of the truck charging. We know a delivery schedule now, and how much charge they take before they return. So we can draw a rough circle around our site to know how far our supply depot might be away if we knew how fast them moved."

"The front of the trucks are covered with dead bugs," Mabel commented off-handedly. She held out a tissue containing a few brightly coloured flakes and wing parts. "Aren't they pretty? I wondered if I could glue some together make a sort of broach. These outfits are just too plain."

A hand reached across the group to gently take the tissue. "These are the elytra of a beetle that infests softwood logs," said the man who took them. "My business was lumber and if these guys showed up, we had to spray the logs." He twisted the tissue so that several of the black scales dazzled in the light. "*Monochamus,* I think is the genus name. This says the truck came from the north, and likely through an area that had a forest fire within the past two to four years that killed the trees these beasties are chewing on. The truck did not come from Toronto. These bugs don't grow there."

"And this wing is likely a Shad fly," the man continued. "Clean water to grow them. This tells me the truck drove overnight – they fly at dusk – attracted to streetlights you know. So that says the highway likely travelled beside a large lake – so it came from the west, probably along the North Channel."

"And that tells me," Harold added, "that this place is likely powered by solar or geothermal. I see no big power transmission towers around so there is likely a solar farm nearby and if not, a bunch of deep holes. If the truck travels by night, it can power up during the day."

"We saw a line of hydro poles running away from the loading area," Mabel offered, "but the insulators were small ones."

"Probably backup power if the batteries are low, or emergency power, but why they'd count on power lines on poles in an emergency is a mystery. They used to be the first to go down in a weather event, as I recall."

"There have to be batteries around if we're on solar."

"Those beetle wings also tell us the truck drove during late day. That's when those things are in flight."

Everyone was talking at once. Irene held up a hand. "I think you guys have forgotten you aren't in your own Board Rooms where everyone else shut up when you spoke." The observation snapped everyone's attention to the fact they'd all been ignoring what each other said. Where it might have caused hostility in an earlier life, they surprised themselves by chuckling in agreement.

"So that truck travelled from late afternoon through dusk and into the night to get here. That gives us a pretty good distance estimate. This truck could have originated from The Sault," concluded Harold into the silence, "if it travelled at about 50 Kph – Thunder Bay if it could double that." Another silence followed.

Irene interrupted. "I'd like to ask a personal question or two. Answer or not, as you wish. I've just been listening to some of the highest paid help in the old world all chipping in ideas to solve a common problem like kids trading player cards. Back then, would you have done that at your club? My experience was that it was put-downs that counted but I haven't heard one. Would anyone care to comment?"

"My Human Resources Head used to talk like that, but you're right. I was pretty demanding, and it was pretty much an echo chamber in the office, if I was really honest. I've overheard other conversations like this before. Is it possible there is another source of chemicals feeding into the supply stream?"

Two others were about to offer their own comments but stopped in mid breath when a quiet thought was offered from the edge of the group. When they realized they'd each given way to the other they chuckled. "I've wondered if what we are showing is a computer effect of delinking and relinking," said the quiet voice.

All eyes turned to him. "I founded the company that made the first Quantum computer – sold out the processes and patents to the guys who built the ones that DL Inc used. Quantum computers have three states. You'd call them 'Yes', 'No' and 'Unknown or Both or even Neither'. The old computers were binary – 'Yes' or 'No' – no in-between. I've wondered since I woke up, if the computer had left the imprint of that third possibility on me, because, like you, I seem to have trouble being certain about anything. If we are all marked by that same lack of single-mindedness, it might just be that we picked up the habit in the computer process – sort of like a watermark on paper that tells where it came from."

"You know that sort of comment back in the day would have driven me crazy. How the Hell do we get anything done? I'd have erupted. Now I wonder why, and the thought of me exploding and waving my arms around, makes me think it happened in an old movie."

"So, we might all now be disabled in some way?" another asked.

"Or newly enabled," suggested the scientist. He shrugged and walked away to be by himself.

*

"I'm afraid to be in the room with a group of them," Mabel confessed. "They're like children each arguing over who has the best trading card, or brutes trying to size up who has to be taken out first." She and Irene had used the droid code to get out of the building and were walking the pathway to the drone landing pad. In the past week, everyone seemed consumed with finding some new informational tidbit to trade. The would-be travelers had found that the only reply they could get about travelling anywhere, was that making the arrangements would take time. The consensus amongst all who had tried was that nobody was going anywhere. They were stuck here.

Which only sharpened the focus on maintaining the supply chain that kept them fed and clothed. Winter would come – then what. Roger seemed to have found a way to loop video of days before 'The Reveal' as it was called, so that any surveillance from afar through closed circuit cameras was derailed. The trucks continued to arrive; food was served regularly in the food court. Some had tried to order sweaters through the normal process and had their requests denied because they were out of season.

"Should we tell them about the trunk room? It would be a supply of other clothes."

"What else might be in those cases - Drugs; the odd pistol or two? I think we should keep that up our sleeve. Look at how people compete when there is nothing really to fight over but rumours," Mabel reiterated.

"Some want to hitch a ride out on the supply trucks but can't figure out how to eat for whatever time that would take. But I expect someone will try it in the next while. After all, most of them were risk-takers in their earlier lives," Irene added.

They'd reached the clearing where the drone had set down that distant day. Mabel's eyes went immediately to the log upon which she usually sat.

"I don't think I ever told you the details of getting that first note," Mabel said. They went towards the log as she went into every item. "And I sat right here and looked down and there... My God. It's back!"

Irene leaned across to look where Mabel was staring.

"Is it the same note as before?"

"The first was gone when I returned the day, they crashed the drone. And this one doesn't have the 'Y' I scratched on the first one either." He picked up the scrap of birch-bark with the new offer scratched into it.

"Help?" the message asked.

"I think we should respond," Irene said. "I am increasingly nervous about remaining where we are. If some do get out on vacations, I would expect that all the chemicals and sedatives we discovered at our site will reappear everywhere else. It is the ideal method of crowd control – especially when you see what's going on around us now. I think it is time to renew our acquaintance with Paul, Peter & Co." With that she pulled out her notebook and tore a page from it. In pencil she wrote: 1.Food for a trip? 2.Rules? 3.Winter?

"Want to offer your scarf to tie it to that sapling?" Irene asked.

"Sure. I can get another, and it will make clear who left the message. On second thought let me tear off a strip. That will still leave me with a backup in case I can't get another." She pulled it free of her hair and was about to tear it. "No wait." She shook her head in confusion. "If I tear it, it's really wrong. Somehow using it for pieces or like a throwaway seems wrong." She tied the note to the tree with the whole scarf, bow bulging like a flower, ends dangling in the breeze.

When they returned the next day, their note was gone. On the ground was another birch-bark patch with the familiar 1,2,3, an arrow pointing down on the first numeral and a box around the last.

"I think we have the makings of high blood pressure here," Irene observed, nodding to the others in the room as they sat chatting with Harold at lunch. They were telling him about the meeting with the Externals day after tomorrow and what they had asked about. "Look at the angst in these faces." She waved at those who nodded at her as she passed. She couldn't recall their names. "Do you think we should all go?" she asked.

"You know if we are the only ones bringing back stories of contact with outside people, we could be accused of making it up," Harold suggested. "I think we need to bring in someone else to the meeting and we don't want to look like a mob so maybe you two and another person from the group. The computer scientist would be my choice."

"I don't think he has the charisma that will connect with most of the others. How about the lumber guy?" Irene offered. "He seems to look for facts."

So, it was agreed that they would invite Bill to meet the Externals.

*

"How do you get out of here?" Bill asked. "The more I look around this place, the more it looks like a prison – a very comfortable but secure prison."

Irene showed him how she used the droid code to open the door then put a stick in the latch to keep it from locking when they closed the door. The delegation was sitting on the log when Mabel, Irene and Bill entered the clearing. Mabel introduced her friends to Peter, Paul and Rachel. Zeke must have been elsewhere.

Rachel was wearing the red scarf Mabel had given her around her hair, flaunting it like a flag. It distinguished her from the others who all wore what looked like a buckskin shirts and long pants. A shift of posture revealed what looked like the second scarf around Peter's waist like a sash or belt.

"This is not the man who helped you collect our food before," Paul observed immediately.

"He is a friend," Mabel explained. "Let me tell you what has happened inside because of the food you gave us." It took a while.

When the conversation turned to their questions, Paul was rather blunt. "We can offer you food for one person for four days for a scouting trip," he stated and handed over four, leaf-wrapped packets. "You need to know that this land only supports a few of us. It is a burden to carry you. Why can't you use your own food?"

"Our food is not preserved. It comes in containers we eat from. There are no covers to carry food, so it won't spill."

"Then you need to dry it to keep it for later."

"We have no fires or driers."

"Then you will have to make them. We can offer you clay pots of live coals to start fires if you cannot start one." That hung in the air for a moment before Irene asked about the rules they follow to survive.

"We all contribute, and we all share, and we take no more than the land can support."

"Who leads you? Who directs or tells the others what to do or not do?" Bill interjected.

The question seemed to puzzle Paul. "We all have special skills or knowledge. It is whoever can best meet the need we have. We honour each other."

"Who would lead you into battle or away from danger?" Bill persisted.

"Who would make war? Don't you know how we got here? Are there not enough daily problems? I don't understand your question."

Irene broke in to get the conversation out of the loop it seemed caught in. "We have tried to get our machines to make us coats, but they don't or won't. We're not sure why."

"In the past," Rachel offered, "there have been no people in your building during the winter. All the people left in big vehicles when the leaves changed colour. There were no trucks travelling in or out during the winter. Nobody was there so why would the machines need to make coats?"

Bill couldn't understand this. "How do you know there were no people there in winter?"

"We could see nobody on the deck, or through the windows. Only in the summer would people reappear. We don't know where they came from because nobody brought them back. The new people were different from the year before and in the fall, they too would leave and not return. It has always been like that since we came here."

"How many others of you are there?" Bill asked.

"Why do you ask?" Peter inquired.

"If we can't stay in our building during the winter, we need to know where we can live."

"Why don't you go away like the others did?"

That question seemed to be the showstopper. "Would you come and talk to our people?" Bill asked.

"I'm not sure what purpose that would serve," Paul concluded, and his companions nodded. "In all the years your place has been here, nobody has come out to us. You all go away, and new people appear – like the ducks."

"It gives a twist to the term 'snowbirds', doesn't it?" commented Mabel. "Maybe we should be going?"

They excused themselves. As she shook Paul's hand, she pressed the small gold coin she'd brought into his palm. He smiled acknowledging the secret exchange.

"Well, that puts a point on it doesn't it," said Bill as they walked back up the path. "We'll be evicted in a while. Where do the new people come from?"

"I expect they are next year's relinks," Irene replied. "Their tissues are likely in culture right now and will be completed during the winter and spring so only a relatively small lab space needs to be maintained at a tolerable temperature. Actually, only the growth tanks need to be heated. The droids could work at any temp."

"So, all we trainees or whatever will be moved to other sites to work or sit around and watch movies? Any bets on the food chemistry to make all that seem like fun?" asked Mabel.

Bill peaked beneath a corner of the leaf wrapping a food packet. "Can you really eat this stuff?"

"We did," Mabel replied. "It is pretty tart, and you don't want to eat too much at once, but it will keep you going. It is really chewy – like jerky or fruit leather. You could probably stretch that out for almost a week if you can get something to drink."

Bill recovered the corner of the food packet without comment.

14

The notice of imminent eviction went through the group like wildfire. Anxiety went through the roof. "Where?" "When?" "With whom?" "I want to stay here!" "They can't make us!" Some remembered roundups from distant days.

"I understand the reason for the medicated existence," Mabel said to Harold and Irene across the table in the Food Court with their own dinner. She was glad that Bill was the center of attention with the news and food packets. "You know you can't help wonder if this doesn't sound like the cleansing of the ghettos and holocaust scenarios."

Harold shook his head. "And to think we all signed up and gave everything we had for this."

Irene set down her coffee and offered a thought. "Well, the other news is that whoever is at the other end of this doesn't seem to know that we know. The question for us is how we, as a collective, and as individuals, will react to the day the food trucks stop or when the buses arrive. Has Roger come up with anything new?" She was looking at Harold for an answer.

"The guy is something else when he gets on a computer and starts messing about. He confirms that the scheduled food trucks have stopped in the past about mid-October and that there is a lot of truck-charging activity about that time. It confirms that people could be moved out. He also found code for minimum level heating etc. for the period after the truck activity. That is likely when the maintenance of all the machinery will happen, and our interventions might be found."

Mabel jumped as a memory came back. "When George and I got here, I met a lady in the lounge who said she and her husband had been farmers. Sold the huge farm that had been in the family for generations to one of those factory farms. I remember she said that they wanted to move back to that community when they relinked and work that land again. They figured they'd look after their own children if they were still around – maybe even grandchildren, who would be seniors by that time. I couldn't understand half her motivation, but it occurs to me that they have the skills that matter to anyone who thinks they might escape to the outside. I remember she said both of them were children of farmers. If anyone knows how to grow food, I'll bet they do. What was her name? I wonder when she decided to come back?"

As she spoke Mabel couldn't help scanning the crowd around the Food Court. *Would she recognize that old lady in her new body now? No face like a poorly plowed field, no arthritic fingers struggling to hold a water glass. Would anyone from that day recognize her?* She sighed at the thought.

The Food Court space was a sea of furrowed foreheads and waving arms. The quiet conversations of earlier days had given way to a discordant crescendo of loud shouts and some wailing. As she got up to return her dirty dishes to the disposal, the couple in the corner caught her eye. The woman was blond haired and broad through the shoulders. Her tablemate, facing Mabel as she crossed the room, was dark haired and blue-eyed and built like a weightlifter. What really caught her attention was their calm set against the darting gestures and table banging in the rest of the room. When she turned the corner and saw the woman in profile, she thought she actually smiled to her companion.

Next morning, as she picked up her breakfast tray and looked for Irene or Harold, it was not the eviction notice that had everyone talking. It was the two suicides of the night before that was being traded in whispers.

Bill caught her as she filled her coffee cup and gave her the details. A young couple had jumped from the verandah to their deaths on the rocks below. They were lying there still. They had to do something.

Harold appeared yawning and stood at the slot from which his breakfast order would appear. They caught his attention as his tray slid out. He joined them at a table where Bill told him about the deaths and that the bodies lay broken and bloody on the rocks below the deck. "We can't just leave them there," Bill declared.

Harold pushed his uneaten food away. "Like what? Do we report them? To whom? Maybe we enter a note on the terminal and wait to see what happens? That seems crass. But we can't leave them there to rot." Everyone was staring at the table and didn't notice the man who had come up behind them.

"You're the man who brought in the food from outside the other night, aren't you," said the quiet voice. They turned. Mabel recognized the husky man she'd noticed at the table with the blond-haired woman the night before. It was his blue eyes that stood out. "And you're the friends of the lady who spoke in the auditorium, are you not?" They all nodded.

"I just heard about the couple who died last night. We were sort of friends with Sam and Cheryl – enough to know their names. Could we get your help to bury them? You knew how to get outside the building to meet those other people. I figured you could do it again. We can't just leave them where they are."

"Where do we bury them?" Bill asked.

"I know a place near the landing pad," Mabel suggested. "It's close by."

"How do we get them there?"

"If we can get into their room, we could use their blankets as stretchers and shrouds," the tall man suggested.

"Irene could probably get into their room," Harold offered. There was silence as they all wrestled with the grisly task before them. "There's Irene now," said Harold, looking up. "I'll get her."

Six of them stood on the path beyond the door. The tall man's companion had joined them. "Emma," she said to introduce herself. "You've met my husband, Günter?" They all exchanged names and handshakes. An awkward silence filled the space between them, each waiting for the others to say what should happen first.

"It has been a long time since I buried someone." Emma said. "Do you think we could get a couple to start digging a grave while the rest of us move the bodies?"

Mabel led them down the path to a small clearing which was deemed suitable. Emma said they'd have to dig with sharp sticks until Harold produced his piece of drone propeller. "That will work well enough to loosen the soil. Maybe someone could work with some bark to scrape the loose dirt away. This will be an all-day job."

Bill quickly volunteered to scrape dirt and move rocks with Harold. The rest set off towards the shoreline. There was no trail; they had to push their way through scrub. When they reached the smashed bodies, nobody looked up. They knew they were the subject of silent scrutiny from the railings above.

Sunlight had dried the blood on the rocks. The drained flesh was grey. They had fallen backwards onto the granite chunks holding each other's hands as they fell. Emma unlaced the entwined fingers and folded Cheryl's arms across her chest. She tipped her sideways while they wiggled a blanket beneath her, then rolled her onto the covering and pulled it up the other side. Mabel did her best to avoid grabbing the blood-soaked clothing. They repeated the process for Sam. They left him in place while they moved Cheryl first. She was closest to the trail they had broken. Moving Sam first would have risked stepping on Cheryl.

With one person in each corner of the improvised stretcher, they began their slow trek back, lifting the body over logs and rocks rather than dragging it, ignoring the buzzing flies and smells that rose up from their load. It was heavy going and they had to stop frequently to rest.

As Emma had predicted it was late afternoon before the bodies were nested side-by-side in the shallow trench that the men had dug in the rocky soil. As she placed one dead hand into that of her companion, Emma removed their identity bracelets from their wrists. Then she reluctantly folded the loose sides of the blankets across each body and stood back. Nobody seemed to know what to do – or were reluctant to start covering the cloth with dirt.

"Gracious Heavenly Father, into your care we commit our friends Sam and Cheryl …," Emma began.

Mabel realized the tears were streaming down her face and she couldn't stop them.

Her prayer ended, Emma, slowly swept her arm across the soil piled beside the pit sending a cascade gently onto the edges of the shroud, then repeated the motion to gradually bury the heads. Each of the others took a turn until the grave was filled. Bill and Harold placed the stones they had dug out of the hole, onto the top.

Irene had worked with Harold's piece of metal to gouge grooves in a birch tree and lever off a plate of bark. She'd written the names of the dead on it with her pencil and then tied it to the cross that Mabel had made of sticks lashed with strips of bark. Dirty and emotionally spent, they climbed the path back to their building as the shadows crept down the hill.

*

At breakfast next day, Mabel sought out Emma and Günter. She noticed how a number of people had already stopped at their table to thank them for so gently taking care of the dead. Most simple touched a shoulder and said, "Thank you". Words seemed to fail everyone. They had all heard about or knew of the improvised burial service from Bill.

When the crowd seemed to disperse, Mabel sat down at their table. "When my husband and I came here I met a woman, I think her name was Emma, in the lounge. That lady said she and her husband were planning to return to the farm they had sold to work and look after their grandchildren. Would that be you by chance?"

"I recall a woman who looked something like you who seemed very angry, but I don't recall her name," Emma confessed. "I do recall that the waitress put a hand-made, crocheted coaster under my drink. It was so well made and so colourful. I used to make them myself but there is nothing here to make them of."

Mabel recalled, in an unbidden flash, how she had set her own glass down on the tabletop where it would leave a mark beside the coaster and regretted the behaviour that the action had unmasked.

"Are you planning to return to your farm?" Mabel asked curiously. This would surely nail the identity of the lady if she were.

Emma looked at her companion. He nodded. "If we're being evicted anyway, yes." She paused wondering if she should reveal all their plans. But carrying out what they had in mind needed the help of the lady with the key.

"Now that we've found you have a way to get out of the building, we'd talked about going out and setting up drying racks to preserve food for travel if we can get your help to go out and in." She didn't reveal that she had used Cheryl's bracelet to get food that morning, so the computers didn't know she is dead. If they could preserve their dead friend's rations, they figured they might have enough food to travel the three weeks they estimated it would take to get back to their old farm.

"How far do you need to travel?" Mabel asked.

"We came from a place west of Toronto north of Kitchener. It was an old German community in pioneer times. We're of German ancestry. If there are people in the forest near here, we would expect there will be neighbours and their descendants where we came from. Blood is pretty…" She stopped in mid-sentence realizing her faux pas.

"When were you planning to leave?" Mabel asked.

"As soon as we could get ready – a couple weeks at most. We'd need to travel while there was enough food to eat along the way to supplement what we could carry. So can we get your help to get out of the building to do food drying?" She looked at Mabel anxiously for a reply.

Emma misinterpreted the extended pause in Mabel's reply. "We can leave our bracelets to let anyone after us use them to get extra food," she hastened to add.

"I was going to ask if we could go with you? There might be some safety in numbers. We have a contact in the locals who might be able to help get us go in the right direction. They might know of dangerous situations along the way." The words were tumbling out. It was Mabel's turn to be anxious. She was hatching this plan all on her own. *What if Irene and Harold didn't want to go? Should Bill be included in the plan?*

"Maybe we should think about this a bit more and meet tomorrow," Emma said.

Mabel readily agreed. When they separated to their regular training duties or whatever, Mabel went to find Irene. Nobody questioned them if they did not stick to the regimen dictated by the lessons. If they didn't learn, they didn't get a certificate and no job. They could always catch up later, but you were lower on a priority list.

When Mabel found Irene, she quickly explained her request to Emma and Günter and asked for the code key to get out and leave a message for their contacts outside. At the log, she scratched a message on bark indicating they sought directions for travelling, and fire, and she boxed the second number in the line. She wanted to see them next day. She tied the bark to the tree with a strip of cedar bark left from the cross she had constructed the day before. When she left, she looked back to see that her note dangled invitingly from the hemlock branch.

When she returned before breakfast next morning, a clay pot of embers sat on sand in front of the log. She left it there and quickly returned to her breakfast appointment. As soon as she said she had fire for a starter, Emma immediately scooped the uneaten meat and bread and butter from her plate and wrapped it in her bandana. "Let's get this train rolling," she said.

Emma showed Mabel how to build a reflector fire so they could hang meat – or whatever it was that looked and tasted like meat - on a skewer and let the fat drip into bread below. "We really need something to seal that food into," Emma observed. "Exposed to the air it will go rancid and smear all over the place. Plastic wrap would do. You didn't come across any bottles hiding along the tunnels anywhere in your explorations?" she pursued.

Startled, Mabel over-reacted in protesting they had found none.

They banked the fire so it would keep going till next day and then sealed their toast soaked in grease between two plates whose rims they sealed with a thin layer of fat. It was immediately obvious that though the air was kept from the food, it wouldn't travel well. As they passed the grave site on the way back, Emma stopped as though in remembrance.

"That was a nice memorial to write their names on the grave," Emma said.

Mabel looked at the inscription anew. She realized it was in pencil. She did not have to look at Emma to realize Emma's comment had been an oblique way of asking the question. "Where did Irene get a pencil?" Emma knew the other women had a secret they were not sharing.

*

"What do you think Harold? Are you in if they'll take us?" Irene asked over the railing on the deck that night as the stars emerged.

There was a long pause before he replied. "No". Mabel was surprised.

"I don't see myself walking for a month to an uncertain welcome. I have a pretty good idea where this leads." He waved his hand around. "There are some computers and AI stuff that is more up my street. There may be drugs at every turn, but digging that hole made an impression on me." He looked down at fingernails still packed with dirt. "No," he repeated "but I suggest you ask Bill. He's lived in the forestry business. He has skills that would be helpful, I'm sure. I just watched the way he worked with me as we dug. He knows that job."

They looked across the water. "You'll need to prepare for winter and rain," Harold added pensively. "Where you want to go there are no thermostats no dry bed at the end of the day. And tomorrow means one more day with a hoe chopping out subsistence from indifferent dirt or marching all day to find what the dirt won't give. No, I'm not going that way."

Irene broke the silence that stretched between them. "We need to know if we're welcome with Emma," Irene concluded. She turned to face Harold. "Thanks, Harold, for your help and pleasure of sharing the time we've had. Go carefully." She shook his hand then Mabel did too. Into the awkward pause Irene turned to Mabel and said, "Let's go."

*

"I don't know if you are prepared for what we're headed into," Emma said with concern as she eyed Irene, Mabel, and Bill. "Have you ever worn anything but high fashion shoes?"

Mabel was both insulted and suddenly afraid. This sounded like she was being kicked off the team. "I played soccer as a teen in my earlier life. I know how to work. But I don't see you offering hiking boots."

Emma's eyes settled on Bill. "I grew up in bush camps. My Mom was a cook, my dad worked on the gang. So did I when I got big enough to swing an axe. I'm no slacker," he said testily.

"Did triathlon when I was in University getting my business degrees," Irene replied quietly and then before tempers shot out of sight, Irene picked up on Mabel's challenge. "She has a point. How do you plan to walk that distance in the slippers we have here." Everyone looked down.

"We'll learn to walk barefoot again," Günter said.

"I doubt it within a couple weeks," Irene commented "and bare feet in winter isn't an option." She paused a moment. "But we might have a source of footwear that will do better." Emma looked up quickly.

"Go on," she encouraged. All eyes were on Irene.

"There is a trunk room full of the stuff that people brought to this place when they arrived to delink. We think it didn't get converted into a file when operating systems changed so it's all been sitting there for about half a century or more. The room isn't even on the maps of the place. There might be shoes, or coats that would serve us well."

"How do we know you aren't making that up?" Günter asked.

Irene held up her pencil. "How do we know you won't steal us blind and then run off?" Both pairs stared at each other. Bill looked from one to the other like he was a referee. Günter broke the silence by holding out his huge hand to shake.
"Because I give my word," he said. "When we promise, we don't go back on it. You sound like you have the right stuff mentally and maybe physically for us all to make a new life if we can work together." Mabel grasped his hand. Irene placed hers on top of the others, Emma added hers to the pile, Bill put his on top.

"I feel like I just joined the Musketeers," Bill quipped.

"I think it's time for some scouting of the resource," Irene said. "Have you got Harold's digger?" she asked Mabel. Mabel nodded.

When Emma entered the trunk room, it was like she'd found Tut's tomb. "Do you think we should touch anything?" she breathed. "This all belongs to other people."

"Well, this case is mine," Irene said leading them to her suitcase.

"And this is mine over here," called Mabel who'd run ahead to get her case open with the hidden key. While she was at it, she opened George's case as well. It wasn't long before the Werner's had located their own travelling bags.

"Take what you think you need for our trip," Günter suggested, "and bring it to the table at the door." Soon they gathered with their stuff.

Emma looked up at Mabel when she dumped George's shoes. "They were my husband's. They fit me if I wear some of his heavy socks. He won't be needing them. I also brought my sewing kit," Emma asked to see it, "and cosmetic case. It has a bunch of bottles you said you wanted for food. I only brought the big two. We'll have to clean them up before we can eat out of them."

"The scissors and needles will be sorely needed," Emma said, "The nail file might be sharpened into something useful. Let me look at the thread." She pulled a loop onto her finger and gave it a tug. "Yes, this is still strong. This is excellent."

When she laid George's woolen lap blanket, fisherman knit sweater and Swiss army knife on the table, everyone looked at them and then her. "George needed to travel with oxygen. We had to cut tubing so that is what he had. I gave mine to our contacts outside." Günter scooped up George's knife to examine which blades it had. "And he always wanted to sit outside, and he always needed these. It didn't seem to matter where we went."

"This can be used as a shawl, coat and sleeping bag," Emma assessed as she flipped it over Mabel's shoulders and checked the fall. "You'll want a big button or two to hold it closed. Add loops on the hem of the blanket, don't' cut a hole. Have you got a belt?"

Mabel only caught the first part. "I don't know how to make a loop."

"I'll show you," Emma said. "Got a belt?"

"Oh yes, lots of belts, but I don't know if they're long enough to go around the outside of this." She appraised her waist size over the blanket.

"I can show you how to put two belts together if you can't figure it out," Günter said.

They looked at Irene's rip stop parka and hood and the Thinsulate boots. "You look good to go," said Emma. Need something for below your waist. Got any rain pants. Or equal?"

Mabel looked down at the high-heeled boots she'd brought from her trunk and suspected they were not worth trying to bring. She remembered George's goulashes in the bottom of his trunk. They would likely be better over his shoes. She looked over at Emma's heavy wool coat and scarf. Günter's was only different in size. Perfectly sensible winterwear. Both had thick boots, but they seemed cracked along the fold lines. 'Age, I guess,' Mabel concluded to herself.

"We'll need to find something for hats." Emma advised, and we need rainwear.

"I saw some big umbrellas on the end of one shelf," Bill offered and hustled off to return with an abundant collection of large ones he'd found.

"Better than nothing," Günter said. "Maybe we could look at the others for just the fabric on them."

The clothes Bill had brought from his suitcase, was his suit coat and pants. "I left all my bush clothes at home when I came here – just brought the business suit I expected to die in till they told me they owned it now and would provide a sheet for delinking."

"Well, he needs more than that," Gunter said pointing at Bill's wardrobe. It begged the next decision.

"I think we should make a list of what we need most and can carry, and then search the other cases for those items. The people who delinked and left them will not likely find them or need them if they do. This stuff will be the difference between survival and not for us."

It was plainly a moral issue for Emma. She reluctantly nodded at the logic, and they started their lists.

*

It was Bill who suggested the solutions to carrying the growing pile of stuff. They had pillaged only part of the cases available and already had more than they could carry. Amongst the many suitcases they found more long coats. By buttoning or zipping them up, they formed a tube that could be stuffed with clothes or medicines they thought they might need. The bottom of the coat was folded up to the yolk and buttoned into loops Emma showed them how to make from the sewing kits and underwear waistbands. The elastic was shot but the synthetic content made it a good choice.

Each learned to sew using the kits that had survived so long waiting to repair a lost button or spilt seam. When they had the looped strip stitched tightly to the yoke of the coat, they added large buttons to hold the hem up. The large buttons were cut from other coats. Then the arms could be stuffed and crossed over the top for additional weather protection and pinned with large safety pins or velcro. Seniors, it seems, travelled with safety pins, or what all the women recognized as blanket pins that held tartan wrap skirts together in their youth. Pack straps were made of the various belts they found and were stitched to the collar of each coat so they could fit over and down the front of the shoulder, around behind the back to tie or buckle in front.

It was also decided to try using some hard-sided suitcases as small sleds to be towed – until they found a wheelchair, then two large wheeled walkers. That set off a pointed search. Eventually they each had a wheeled wagon they thought would get them over bad ground onto roadways. Hard-sided suitcases might double as sleds if they were towed on their sides by a belt attached around the handle.

They placed a priority on medications they found. Some were unknowns but most recalled anti-inflammatories. They recognized sleeping pills and medicine for constipation and diarrhea. They figured the antiseptics and antibiotics were probably ineffective anymore but not the pain meds. They probably still worked. They found lots of them.

All tools like scissors or jack-knives, and sewing kits were collected. One person had a watercolour field kit and sketchbook. Irene decided to find a place she could carry that. The jewelry went into a pile they decided might be trade goods if they could carry them. It was the bird books and the accompanying two pairs of binoculars in the luggage of one couple that was judged the best find.

"Were they planning to bird watch?" Bill asked. "I thought most were in wheelchairs or had eye problems that would leave them blind."

"Hence the equipment for alternate activity," Irene commented. "I'll bet they were birders from the get-go and these things never left their suitcase. Probably had a second set in the glove box of their car."

They failed to find something that would serve as a pot for food preparation on the way but the bottle request for food storage was filled with personal water bottles. Many were plastic and could hold everything they wanted to pack in it. There was a bunch of metal water containers that Emma decided might serve as individual serving vessels instead having a communal pot. They could be heated in a fire with the ration for that meal and then used for other purposes later.

There were a surprising number of cutlery kits. It set off a discussion of early days in a previous youth of travelling on foot, buying bread, wine and cheese in a village and eating it in a park. Irene recalled being chased out of such a place in Monte Carlo where she'd taken her sandwich from the meal pack provided on the tour bus, because the gardener thought she looked like a vagrant. "If he could see me now," she quipped as she shrugged into her pack to test the straps.

"How many million did you trade for this trip?" Mabel asked of the group.

"Wisdom of hindsight. Priceless!" grumbled Bill.

"You're going to have to change your attitude, if you want to survive," Emma chided. "Here you have a whole new chance to create a new beginning that won't lead to a world like the one we just left. Of all the people left on earth, there are only a few who know how that world came to be, how we got to be so rich at the expense of those who couldn't. How we burned the country to the roots physically and figuratively. Surprisingly we're on the same footing as all those others who survived by luck or whatever, but they don't know how it happened. We do because we made it. So, our first job is to survive, and out next job is to influence the new generation."

"So where do I get my superhero shirt?" asked Bill.

"Check some of the other trunks. I think I saw one over there," Irene said with a straight face.

Their sorting and pack construction took place mostly after supper. During the day those who weren't busy with the outside fire, were collecting firewood. When they came for meals, it was a quick dash into the Food Court at the beginning of a meal so they weren't closely observed, by others, putting food claimed with the bracelets of the two suicides into their book bags, along with any declared excess from their own trays. That sort of activity would have led to unwanted questions. As each person filled his pack and wagon, they moved them to their fire area where they set them under secured umbrellas. When their improvised efforts proved resistant against even heavy rains, they were really quite proud. Even the clay pot of coals had survived.

Paul and his clan had shown them how to make fire with flint and steel and also with a fire bow. After that lesson, they might know how to do it but hoped they never had to demonstrate it again. They had been taken on walks to learn the wild foods they could eat and how to snare small animals. They traded a wheelchair that Irene had turned sideways and improvised into a potter's wheel as return for the training in how to make clay vessels – if they could get clay. They already had the ability to fire clay.

Paul said they had traded with a group further south for their supply of powdered clay and that technology. Irene revealed she had learned the skill of making pottery in her youth at a girl's camp.

They guessed it was mid-August. They had noticed the invitation posted from Harold on their room screens, to come and observe the Perseid meteor shower a couple nights earlier. That only happened in early or mid-August, Mabel and Irene remembered from their earlier reading. So, when they finally decided they were as ready as they could be, they agreed to leave the next day. Paul said they would walk them south and point them in the right direction.

Because they had been so involved with their preparations, they were surprised at what mealtimes and after-dinner meetings on the deck or auditorium had become. "Haven't seen you around much," Harold greeted when he saw them at what they planned was their last dinner.

"Finishing up our training sequences," Irene answered for them. Bill and the Werner's were with other groups.

Harold thought about that a moment and nodded.

"It sounds a lot noisier in here than it used to," Irene observed.

Harold chuckled. "Well, I suppose that when you put so many entitled people together and take away their meds, one shouldn't be surprised if there is more than enough bickering. Every gathering is a lobbying opportunity for one faction after another to persuade everyone else. I suppose the only thing that saves us from armed combat is lack of weapons and what I'll call the quantum effect – that feeling of ambivalence we all seem to have. People still hold strong opinions and think that they have an ultimate and reasonable solution for everyone to follow, and which they will personally lead. But if anyone wants to stop the parade, he shouts out "are you sure?" That usually results in a lot of profanity and a challenge to suggest a better plan but it hasn't come to blows yet. Close, but no punches. And we all get three meals a day, a warm bed and shower each night, perpetual health care, and all the movies we can watch.

"Do you wonder when it will stop?" Irene asked.

"Roger has found out to the day when the trucks arrive to move us out. We figure we can take over as soon as we get to a terminal on the other end. Roger has found a way into secure files using the vehicle maintenance programs."

"If he did, maybe someone else did and is waiting?"

"Well from everything we see, the system is designed to perpetuate itself and those it looks after. People like us seem to fill the blanks by providing the odd behaviours or asking the peculiar questions that the system then learns from. So, this looks like the world I left."

"Have you found out how the supply chain runs?" Irene asked. "How does it fix itself when a shortage develops or a disaster, like weather, wipes out a part of it?"

"Haven't found any such records."

"Everything recycles," Harold continued, "and with enough energy, the systems seem to make more of what it needs. Looks like perpetual motion – but of course energy keeps it going."

"And one hundred percent recovery of every resource?" Irene asked.

"Must be."

"Ice Storms or tornadoes don't pull down the wires?"

"They must be underground, or the energy source could be geothermal. Seems to me I recall that being mentioned when we signed up."

"You thought you'd found financial indications that a war might be going on."

"I thought that originally but now I don't know. There are units that just disappear, but I've got no idea why. I've wondered if they are operating under another system, and I haven't found the link. Anyway, I don't lie awake wondering about it."

"Is there any indication of people other than ourselves - the relinked ones – in the system?" asked Mabel.

"Well, it is a business, Mabel," Harold offered a bit condescendingly. "It looks after its own liabilities and operating costs. Yes, it is a big business, but it doesn't do head counts or costs of supplies beyond its own needs. And secondly, DL Inc. is an entity with a duty to survive. So, it does what any business does to compete and continue."

"Is there any indication of changes in the liabilities of DL Inc. – that it might be taking on more clients or that relinking is increasing?"

"Both are trending downward slowly currently but it seems that coming back a century after delinking had some sort of attraction so there is a projected big bump in a couple decades."

"To whom does DL Inc. pay taxes?"

"Government of Canada, so I guess there is a national government."

"That is not obvious from our conversations with the locals," Mabel interjected.

Harold just tossed up his hands. Into the silence that followed, he pressed the women on their decision. "Are you sure you want to leave. You're stepping off a cliff here. No health care, no pension plan, no meal plan. You got to admit the room and board isn't too bad."

Mabel and Irene looked at each other and then at Harold. Irene spoke for both. "It is a dead-end street, Harold. It is committed to perpetuating a lifestyle that caused the misery of the rest of the world. What DL Inc represents, I expect, to any outside survivors, is an enormous treasure trove waiting to be pillaged when they have the strength to do so especially when DL wants what the outsiders' resources for their ultra-rich clients in forts like this."

"Well, I guess we can agree to disagree then."

"Thanks for the company and the memories, Harold. Maybe we'll meet again." Irene said.

"Sounds like you're planning your exit soon," Harold deduced.

They all stood and shook hands silently.

Next morning, the travelers met after breakfast at their fire circle where all their gear was ready. While waiting for the Werners, Irene went back and closed the door completely. She heard the lock click. Then she waved the robot code across the sensor they had found outside the door and heard the latch release. The Werner's arrived at that moment. "What is that about?"

"Just checking that it works. I wonder for how long?"

Paul and Peter arrived as arranged and the caravan set off.

At the first rest stop, their guides said they would be leaving. They had come out onto the top of a huge rock cut through which a roadway stretched southward before them. Paul cautioned them about getting too hot. "It might be better to rest till after dark and travel when it is cooler," he cautioned. "It will be very hot today. Be ready for storms in no more than three days."

"You have been good friends," Irene said. "I don't know if we can repay you." Irene stood facing their benefactors and made a decision. She was going to hand over all their bracelets but at the last moment she separated out their own. Maybe this was their backstop. Maybe they'd be written off whatever computer record but as long as they were in hand, she felt there might be somewhere back into the safety of the society they were choosing to abandon. Was it a faint hope clause or Hail Mary hope? Whatever it was, she pocketed their own ID's.

Instead, she held out the bracelets of the two suicides along with a floor plan of the facility on one of her note pages. "You might impersonate them for a while and get access to food or clothes or whatever else. Stay in their rooms or go to the food court only when you won't be observed. The map shows the tunnels used by the droids. This code waved in front of the sensor should get you in the door we used." She handed him the Identification tags.

Paul accepted the tags uncertain what they really could do. "You are a target for anyone who would steal your things," he said. "I know you think there are friends where you came from and I hope you are correct, but there are many dangerous people between here and there. Travelling after dark will protect you from most. Be sure to look ahead before you go into open spaces."

"Do you have a mailing address, or do we just use your email?" quipped Bill. "We'll let you know when we get there."

"Pardon," asked Peter, puzzled.

"Never mind," said Mabel. "It's a secret joke."

"Go carefully," the guides said in farewell. As they shook hands, Bill held up his hand in the Vulcan salute. "Live long and prosper," he said.

Peter laughed and asked how he kept his fingers like that. They had struggled down the hillside to the road. When he turned around Bill could still see Peter was trying to master the finger arrangement and laughing as he shouted, "Live long and prosper."

After an hour of hiking on the pavement with full packs and wagons in the sun and sticky air, they decided it was likely better to move after the heat the day. They slid down the embankment and took shade in a large culvert through which a trickle of water ran. Everyone was pack-sore and exhausted. A truck rumbled by overhead reminding them that they were not pioneers. Others lived around here. They would be crossing space that others claimed. They would be invaders, interlopers, refugees, or travelers. But what they walked on, they did not own, and they had to face the various responses they might face if they confronted other people.

15

It took two days, well nights really, to reach a bridge over broad water with the vastness of Georgian Bay visible to the west. "I know this place. We stopped here to eat our lunch when we came up," Günter said as though it was last weekend. Knowing they were going the way they wanted lifted everyone's spirits. The diner they had eaten in was just a pile of collapsed rubble.

They had developed a pattern to their progress. First, they studied the roadway they hope to travel with their binoculars to decide if there were outposts where people might be watching. If they found none, they moved as far as they had searched and then looked again. Only once did they spot a sentry and he left at sunset. They were happy to pass that outcrop in the dark.

Trucks were obviously linking distant points but there were not many. They seemed to travel on a predictable schedule and the howl of their tires could be heard at a distance. They were not lighted though. Lights were needed for human drivers. Those guiding these machines obviously were not.

So, when they learned to expect the trucks, they kept a sharp ear out and got off the road in good time. Mabel's sky studies stood them in good stead. She had pointed the Pole Star out to everyone and how it would not move while the rest would appear to. "Keep that to our back and we're headed where we want to go, Emma," she advised.

"Good," was the reply. "And if we can't see it?"

"Other stars can give us direction, but you need to know they rotate around the Pole Star during the night. They only seem to move counterclockwise if you're looking north" Mabel said, with pride.

"But if you can't see the Pole Star, how do you know which way to face. If you were looking south under a cloudy sky, the few stars you might see would be moving clockwise, and to get them rotating the way you said, you'd find yourself walking north, back the way we came, said Emma with continuing confusion.

"So, you need to know what the constellations look like, or you find the rock I left on the path before we camped. I always leave a rock a little further south of where we turn off the road." Mabel said with a smile. Everyone laughed.

"I guess you need to be our age to know what a clock was to know which way the hands went," observed Bill. "I wonder if such an instruction would be of any use to anyone raised on a digital clock?"

Irene marched on in silence towards the place they would stop and check the road ahead. The late-rising moon that had cast only a slight glow through a high sheet of cloud was giving way to dawn. It would soon be time to camp for the day. From the heat and humidity already, it would be another scorcher of a day. Best to be somewhere cool.

Irene found the repetitiveness of marching and pushing her wheelchair of belongings both meditative and metaphoric. Walking was boring and it made you sore. The squeak of old wheels was hypnotic. It was easy to fall into wondering what she had done. Why was she really walking down this highway in the wilderness? She had committed herself to a complete unknown for what? Was it all about nobody telling her what to do – some sort of ego trip? She had just walked away from a lifetime of idle comfort because…? She just couldn't grasp her reasons anymore. It was as if finding the others who were of like mind had given her a sense of belonging, she didn't feel back at the Relink Centre. Back in the concrete bunker might be all life's comforts but the more she thought of it, the more it felt and sounded like a prison. So, was she now in a box constructed of expectations instead of stone? This was too much.

She listened to the quiet chatter of the others. It filled the time. She couldn't contribute to the idleness of it. It only made her feel frustrated that she could not see the importance in discussing the obvious. She should have been paying attention to their surroundings, she realized too late when three armed men stepped into the roadway ahead of them. She turned to run but another was behind them. They had just stepped into an ambush.

"Look what we have here" said a deep male voice sarcastically. "It looks like the supply train that we thought was coming earlier got held up. Good to see you finally made it."

Their group closed ranks.

"Over there," said the leader and tipped his rifle towards a faint track through the roadside weeds.

*

Later, when Mabel let the memory slip up through the layers under which she had buried it, she did not recall all, but still too much, about the assaults. They were within a clearing within sight of the road. She remembered three trucks speeding by in convoy. She recalled the sound of the thud of a rifle butt against Günter's head while Emma was screaming and struggling to hold the barrel. When Günter went down, she covered him with her body howling hysterically. Mabel thought she was kicked before the assailant went after their baggage. She didn't see the boot-kicking that left Bill insensible.

The next image Mabel recalls if she can't help it, is the thieves dumping their packs and wagons, kicking aside the clothes, and snatching up the bottles of medicines. She remembers them demanding to know what the bottles of medications were. Mabel remembers being on the point of telling the one thug when Irene had shouted not to tell what the one in his hand was. It earned her a clout on the side of the head and several more slaps across the face till she said it was Viagra – an aphrodisiac. "With one of those, you could have sex all day."

That was when the fight broke out between the robbers. The bottle arced away pills flying through the air as each punched and pushed to get it. The men scrambled after them snatching them up and swallowing them as soon as they found one after another. As the turmoil developed, Irene had backed Mabel into the brush and picked up a branch for defense. Taking her lead, Mabel picked up a rock. As she did, a phrase from one of those movies they had watched a month earlier bubbled up in her mind. "Don't bring a knife to a gunfight," the actor had said. Here she and Irene were with a stick and a stone against four men with rifles.

The scramble ended with the four assailants, leaf litter and twigs sticking out of their beards standing across the littered clearing from the women, swaying on their feet. The leader raised his rifle, and it wove a figure eight in the air. "I'm ready," he slurred. "Get over here."

Irene theatrically threw down her branch. "Let me make up a bed," Irene stalled and bent to pick up coats to make a mattress and moved to his right. Mabel looked at the others. One sagged against a tree and slid slowly down it into a heap. The other two were watching their leader's advance on Irene. Mabel moved to the left.

Irene distracted the men with a hypnotic and slow start to a strip tease - enough for Mabel to circle behind them. One brute seemed to lose interest as he staggered off towards his own pack. Mabel beaned another with her rock, and he went down. The leader lurched for Irene who sidestepped, nimble as a ballerina, snatched away his rifle, spun around and using the gun as a bat, hit the thug's head with a grand slam swing. Mabel could recall the sound of that 'Whack' and the thump following it whenever she heard a door slam in later life.

Irene then turned for the last assailant who, by then, had fallen down by himself. When she realized he was no threat, she dropped the gun and turned to Emma.

"Well, they looked like Viagra," Irene splat out satirically later, when they sat later trying to gather themselves. "They're little blue pills – right? How was I to know they were sleeping pills?" By the time they had revived Bill and Günter, tended to their wounds and repacked their gear, at the drugged attackers had stopped breathing. The women had collected the weapons and added them to their carts. Günter had to be wheeled in one of their wheelchairs he was so groggy. Bill, despite his pain, insisted on trying out the rifles to see if they worked. Irene's example was not enough. It was old ammunition after all. "It's necessary to be sure each one works," Bill had insisted. He tried each weapon on the man who had held it and beaten him to the ground. Each rifle left a neat hole in its owner's head where a third eye might have been. It was not the only mutilation Mabel had considered.

Emma had walked away from the slaughter pushing Günter. Bill caught up in a while with the useful clothing the men had worn along with the gun-cleaning kits and ammunition from their packs. Mabel had loaded Bill's gear on hers and was pulling his wagon as well. Nobody could bear the thought of eating off the metal dishes and pots the men had had. "I left them beside the naked corpses," Bill spat when he joined them.

Emma recalled that they should not travel further south on the main road a short time after they had left their infamous stop. "We have to turn southwest on that road over there," she pointed. That is southwest, isn't it?" she asked as she pointed. Mabel turned to check her directions.

"Right," she said.

As they walked that night, the sheet of cloud of the day before became a lower slab through which the moon could not shine. Around midnight, they had to find shelter. Ominous lightning flashes on the horizon added urgency to their search. Instead of refuge in a ditch, they found shelter in a metal shed. Bill shot off the sensor and latch on the side door. Inside there were a dozen robots like the Cameronbots they had left. It was the green lights on control panels that gave the first indication of their presence.

In lightning flashes that were almost constant, they could see the machines were lined up like posts with an appendage connecting each to some sort of tube that ran down the middle of the barn. They didn't need light to know the other contents of the barn. The smell was strong and sweet. Beside them were large crates of apples. Being in the scented air seemed to revive Günter a bit, but he still complained about a huge headache.

Then came the rain – rivalling the sound of the thunder as it poured down on the galvanized roof. The door began to slam back and forth, having lost its latch. The building shuddered as gusts and limbs hit the sides. Another roaring arose over the rain; the door disappeared, ripped away. The travelers huddled between the bins as first one sheet of roofing tore away, then a second. The roaring subsided under the pounding sound of the rain again. Spray forced them into a more protected corner. Huddled together, they waited for the storm to pass and when it was a distant rumble, they fell asleep. When they awoke, aching and cramped, the sun was high, and the air was cool and sweet. *

*

It was obvious that they needed to stop for that day. The men were so sore from the beatings they had taken. Günter probably had a concussion; Bill surely had broken ribs.

Outside away from the blank stares of the bots without even their green indicators now, the women started a fire. Emma organized the slicing of apples for drying It took a while to get the apple branches that had blown down and rolled like tumbleweed into the side of the building in the storm, burning. Emma suggested the smoke might add a desirable flavour. It was making virtue from their adversity. They all knew that, but it was better than moping.

The storm had torn a swath out of the countryside several hundred meters wide. The track of destruction had passed slightly north of their shelter. Mabel and Irene went off to see the damage after scrutinizing the area with binoculars.

The effect of the storm was horrifying. Any tree that stood was stripped and stark. "It's because they all came rolling our way," Mabel suggested. From some high ground, they could see what had been a farmhouse on the edge of the path of destruction. It was simply a foundation covered by wreckage. "Wonder if anyone was living there?" Mabel asked aloud.

Irene was studying the remains of a barn nearby with binoculars. It was leaning dangerously but was looking better than the house. Down the wind Mabel thought she could hear bird sounds.

"I don't see any movement at the house but if they were injured, they might not be able to be active. I think we should have a look there before we go back."

"Are you sure you want to do that. Our last visit with people wasn't so good."

"Those were animals, not people. I refuse to think of the world like that. And I brought this." Irene pulled a pistol from her pack. "It was in the belt of the one with the big gut," Irene said. She turned the black thing back and forth so Mabel could see all sides. It sucked the light from the air.

There was no way to creep up on the wreckage that had been a house, but they found themselves bent over as though there was a hedge to hide behind. They found a woman and a man skewered and crushed by falling timbers in what must have been the bathroom. An outside wall had collapsed after the roofing had fallen like spears into the space. It formed a tent over the bathtub and the smashed bodies. They both shook their heads. Mabel thought of Sam and Cheryl, splayed out on the rocks as she caught sight of a ruined face through a space in the boards.

"I don't see how we can bury them," Mabel said. "There is just too much to move to get them free. Maybe we can just cover them with scraps."

Their conversation was broken by animal sounds from the barn. "Go and see what is there," Irene directed. "I'll cover up these people."

Mabel walked carefully to the barn that was sagging sideways. It was a bank barn. Earth had been heaped up on three sides giving a ramp up which a wagon could be hauled to load the second level and a haymow above it. On the fourth side, the lowest level, like a basement of the barn, let out into a corralled yard deep in mud. The rest of the barn tilted over the space precariously. Three chickens were pecking about the puddles at insects that seemed to be there.

Mabel was wondering how she could catch them when a bleat came from inside the barn. There was a wide doorway from the penned yard into the barn. The doorway had Dutch doors. The upper one was jammed tight but with pulling, she thought she could open the lower door enough. She went looking for an easier way. Flanking the doorway were windows to each side, covered with shutters. She couldn't get them open. 'Must be clamped inside," she concluded. It was back to the door.

Repeated yanking opened the lower door enough that she could crawl through. Continued bleating encouraged her. She came up, wet-kneed, in the gloom inside. A squawk of chickens from the aromatic darkness accompanied her arrival.

Immediately inside the door, on her left, was a railing about chest high. If she clambered over it, she reasoned, she could get to the shuttered window around which light seeped. She did so, stepping into something soft and smelly. At the window she knocked up the bar closure silhouetted in the space between the shutters. The shutters swung into the yard flooding the pen she was in with southern sunshine. She turned from the brightness outside to see four long faces quietly staring at her from the corner where the outside stone walls met. One bleated a challenge. She took a step towards the group. While the noisy one stamped a foot, the other three scooted to the other furthest corner.

Mabel got the message. She backed carefully to the railing and climbed up, hooking her heels into the bars so she didn't have to turn around. The quiet goats returned to a thread of grain that was sifting down in a thin stream from the ceiling. They jostled for it amidst the straw in the pen.

Safely over top of the railing and watching the goats, Mabel stepped down the outside of the railing to the doorway and was scared out of her wits by a sudden snort in her ear. She screamed and jumped back up the fence and turned to her assailant. Large brown eyes and long black snout leaned out of the gloom and across another fence to the right of the doorway and snorted again.

Mabel melted with relief. It was only a horse. She reached out to pat it and it rubbed against her hand. In a few minutes, she had decided it was docile enough and had climbed the barrier into its box stall and opened that window also. More light flooded into the space bringing cool air as well. The freshness accented the pungent ammonia smell of the space she was in.

Through the window, Mabel saw Irene headed her way with a bundle of blankets in her arms.

Always can use blankets these days, she thought. She called out to Irene, "Come see what's here."

While Irene approached, Mabel looked around the newly lighted barn space. There were four stalls. She was in the one with the horse. Behind it was another stall with a black-andwhite face staring over the rail and another small face looking between the lower bars. In the back corner behind the goat pen, were four smaller goats. In the space between the back pens, at the end of the corridor from the doorway, was a collection of boxes, open-end facing outward, where the chickens obviously lived.

She turned back at the sucking sound of Irene approaching through the mud of the paddock. "Come in through the window," Mabel called.

"Can you help?" came the reply.

The horse was looking out her window at Irene so Mabel could not see her right away. She got to the horse's side and was about to tell her of her discoveries when Irene held up the bundle of blankets. From it stared the wide blue eyes of a baby about one year old. The child held out its arms to Mabel.

"Oh my god," Mabel said, enfolding the child who was crying for comfort. She held the child tightly trying to make soothing sounds.

"In the bathtub," Irene said.

"What do we do with it?"

"I was thinking we could barbeque it or maybe sell it," Irene said sarcastically. "What do you know about baby care?"

"I spent my whole earlier life avoiding it. Had a brother with kids. HIs example was reinforcement to my choice not to."

"Looks like you're calling on lost skills now," Irene commented and then added. "I was infertile. At least that was the diagnosis and why I spent my whole life building a multi-million-dollar career."

"To think," Mabel added, looking at the child in wonder, "I had to live to be a hundred in order to have a child. Well, it's just a rental." The baby had stopped crying and was studying her intently. "I gather nobody else was alive," Mable surmised.

"What you see is what you got." Irene replied.

Irene entered as Mabel had but stayed in the middle corridor. "These animals have feed in their mangers and water troughs are full," she said. "The farmer obviously set them up well for the night, but I don't like the idea of them being in the place if this barn falls down. Let's try to get the doors open so we can get them into the paddock."

Mabel took the baby out to the yard. She unwrapped the infant to find the child was double-sweatered under a long nightgown and wore a thick white diaper. In the distance, Irene bashed out the Dutch doors with a timber. Then she used long leather leads hanging on a hook to snag the halters of the horse and cow and lead them out where she tied them to posts supporting a roof over a covered manger and water trough. The calf followed along.

"What about the goats?"

"I think they're separately penned for a reason, but I don't know what it is, but I'll bet Emma does. She's the farm girl here."

Baby was getting fussy and smelly. "Did you find anything to change the baby with?" Mabel asked.

"All I can suggest is wrapping her in one of those blankets. I think that if you can take her back to Emma while I look around to see if I can find clothes or diapers or whatever, and then bring Emma and the men here, that would be the best way to spend the rest of the light we have."

"Emma probably knows what to feed the child."

"Hey," Mabel said. "Those young goats are separated from their mothers. I'll bet there is a reason. I'll bet the nannies are supplying milk. Ever milk a goat?"

"I presume that is rhetorical."

"Here. You clean up baby and I'll try to get some milk for her. There is a mug and small pail hanging on a spike in the barn. I wondered what it was for."

Mabel was somewhat successful. One nannie's teats were dripping milk her udder was so swollen. It did not try to run when Mabel caught it and tied it closely to the rail inside its pen. It took a little imagination to figure out how to increase the flow, but Mabel was successful and poured a full cup from the pail before that goat kicked it over.

Irene improvised a way to get milk into the baby without too much spilling down her chin.

"We've lost an hour," Irene complained. "You keep baby here. You've already figured out how to feed her and I'll run back and bring the others. I can go faster by myself."

Before she could argue, Irene had jammed the child back into Mabel's arms and was jogging away.

"How do you do anything else when you have a baby to care for?" Mabel wondered. As she re-inspected the barn, she found a ladder that let down from the ceiling over the central corridor and the steps took her up to the hay and feed stored above. It was obvious when she got there that it was hay holding the barn up. It was stuffed to the roof, which seemed intact. It was also obvious that she could do little carrying a baby in her arms.

She returned to where she'd dropped her pack, removed the contents and reversed the fold so it was against her back. Baby slid in like a pole in a hole. She left the arms dangling and swung it up onto her back. Baby made happy babbling sounds – must have liked the view.

With Baby in her pack on her back, Mabel returned to the barn and forked a pile of hay down the stairs using a long-tined tool hanging on a post at hand. When she got down to the stable again, she divided the feed up among the animals. She had no idea how much each should get but if they didn't like what she offered, she told them they could fill out a complaint form. She took the last of what she'd brought down to the manger out in the paddock. It had been blown clean by the storm. Baby had not stopped wiggling the whole time. She even figured out how to turn around to look forward over Mabel's shoulder or back the way they had come.

Thoroughly weary, Mabel wandered, with baby, off towards the house to see if there was anything she could find that might be useful to them. *Something to feed a baby with would be good*, she thought.

Before dark, Mabel had found several blankets stuck on brambles in the lea of the barn. She never did get to the wreckage of the house. It took a long time to slowly pick the bedding loose without too much tearing. Then it was time to feed baby again, and herself. She got the three nannies to deliver a whole pail full and managed to put her foot in place so that goat could not kick the pail at all. She had decided to bed down in the haymow above the stable. That's where she was, with the baby and the tattered blankets, when she heard the calls outside as Emma and the rest arrived. 'God what will I do if it's another bunch of thugs,' she thought at the first hail. Her relief was euphoric when they called her name.

Emma and Günter both surveyed the barn in the fading twilight and declared it safe enough to sleep in, so everyone bedded down in the hay for the night. Baby woke everyone at first light. Mabel was delegated to milk the goats again. She led them out one at a time on a tether then let them loose into a more distant enclosed part of the paddock. Emma told her that was obviously the outside goat pen. What made it so was a mystery to Mabel.

Günter was obviously feeling much better after a day's rest and sleeping in the hay. He was positively animated. Emma and he scampered around the site like mice. This was their element. Bill was pleased to supervise and carry messages. Lifting was too painful to do; laughing was excruciating.

Together, they all could lift the debris and extricate the dead bodies.

After burial, the group set about scavenging the wrecked home and bent barn.

By mid-day, Günter and Emma had located but left in place, two wagons that Mabel had not found because they were behind a wall of hay. They had to open the barn doors at the top of the ramp on the backside of the building to get to them. Obviously the farmer had started filling the barn at the top of the ladder and worked towards that door. With the barn full, there was just enough room for the wagons inside the big doors.

There were two sizes of wagon: one fit under the other. Fortunately, Günter was able to recognize the harness needed to hook up animals to them. That's when he deduced that the cow must pull the smaller wagon. Günter felt there should be other implements, maybe buried in the hay along the walls. They would be exposed as the hay was used during the winter so by next spring, they would be available for use.

The farming couple also recognized the sacks of grain – corn, oats, wheat – in the corner over the goat pen that served as a granary. When they discovered the grain, they counted, looked at each other and went on with their inventory.

Mabel found that Baby was only content to stay in his backpack carrier for so long. She was just as glad; the child got heavy after a while. But where do you put a baby in a wrecked building? To remove the bodies, the group had moved a lot of debris. Mabel cleared a pen for the child on the house's floor. Baby was pleased to crawl about on the gritty space and stand up against the improvised barricade. Mabel was delighted by the show of skill and cheered. The child dropped to the floor and crawled to the other side of her space, stood again, and looked back while putting a finger into her gooey mouth. "How old are you, baby dear?" asked Mabel to her drooling companion. "What is your name?"

Because it kept her within quick reach of the child, Mabel took over scrounging what might be buried in the debris of the house. Her search yielded a woodstove for cooking, battered chimney pipes, a whole cupboard full of preserves and dry goods that had been protected by roofing that slanted over it, and the kitchen hand pump. When they cleared the debris around, it still pumped water. They sat around on whatever was available for a mid-morning drink. The treasure, as far as Mabel was concerned, was a bureau that had stood its ground against more fallen timbers and delivered a drawer full of clean, dry flannelette diapers, a clay pot of what looked like Vaseline ointment, four large safety pins and three sets of canvas overalls that would fit the child for a while. The joy in her voice as she announced the discovery against the silence of the others, was tacit agreement that Mabel had just become the surrogate Mom.

They all sat in a circle at dinner on the cleared floor of the house. What did you do with such wealth suddenly dropped in front of them? Emma still held reservations about appropriating anything that really belonged to others. The discussion revealed how quickly the 'Finders Keepers' mentality had resurfaced. There seemed no outside authority to enlist to solve the problem.

"What problem," Bill persisted. "They died. We buried them as best we could. We showed the respect they deserved and that we could offer. Their stuff is ours now. If we do nothing, this all goes to waste and heaven knows it may save our skin." Nobody tried to rebut the argument.

Baby was crawling around in the circle to each person, standing and pulling on beards or hair. Baby's age came up again. Emma's suggestions were accepted as gospel.

"Four top teeth and four bottoms say she is just over a year. If she hasn't walked yet watch out. She will be soon, and we can probably serve her soft foods."

"What are soft foods?" Mabel asked.

"Applesauce and stuff like it. If we can find a grinder, we could grind up some of the oats we found in the barn and make her porridge. Cheese if we could make the goat's milk into it. Or you could chew up some of our dried meat into a paste and try her on that." Before Mabel had a chance to respond to that idea, Emma continued. "Did you find any kitchen equipment like pots, pans, utensils?"

"I set out whatever was under the sink." Mabel nodded to the far side of the cleared floor. The baby was playing with them. There was a small axe under the wood stove with the firewood," Mabel said quickly and then before anything else came up she said, "We can't keep calling her Baby. She needs a name."

Everyone offered names of female relatives. Emma suggested the one that everyone agreed to, especially when she gave the Germanic meaning of the name – water sprite.

"Good, Emma," said Irene. "I did find her in a bathtub after a rainstorm. Seems right. Nixie it is." And then she went on.

"I'm going to make a list of the tools and stuff we take from here. Like it or not we have become Nixie's guardians and personally I live in hope that we will find a new place to live and where she can grow up. She may even get to be as old as we are." Everyone laughed and disagreed with that.

"But if and when she decides to move out on her own," Irene continued, "I think she should be able to claim these items or items like them, as her …. What's it called?"

"Trousseau," said Emma.

"Dowry," said Günter.

It was a skillful invention that got past Emma's reservation, and everyone agreed. Mabel caught the mouthed 'thank-you' across the circle from Emma to Irene.

"As long as we're naming things," Bill said, "I vote to call the horse, 'General'. He's got a star on his chest, so he has to be a big shot. He gets to lead us and take the blame if something goes wrong." That brought a laugh and started off the evening's entertainment - naming the animals. Everyone was in such high spirits, that Günter was reluctant to throw a damper on things, but, prodded by his wife, he finally did.

"Think about this a bit," he asked. "We have to move on. We've about a hundred and fifty clicks to go – at least ten days good walking. The animals represent a problem as well as benefits. Their food for a winter is here." He nodded towards the barn and his arm swept the partially ruined pastures. "If we leave them here alone, they might survive a while. Maybe someone else will find them. Who knows?"

"If we take them with us, we can't carry enough feed for them to survive the winter. Assuming we can find a place to stay ourselves where we hoped, we cannot assume that there will be space or feed to keep this bunch alive. Even pasturing them outdoors till the snow flies will not work. The plants they would eat don't re-grow in cold weather. Keeping them on grass longer means they eat up what they'd start on in the spring. Sheltering them through the winter is just slow starvation." The mood had dropped heavily.

"So, while I think we should take them with us, I want you all to know that they cannot all be sustained until the Spring. It might be best not to become too attached to them."

They all went off to bed in the barn starkly aware of the precariousness of their position and that of their new companions.

*

It was a week before they were on the road again. They looked like a caravan. Günter had found the racks that fit into the sockets on the sides of the wagon so they could pile it high with hay – on top of the wood stove. Tools filled the firebox and ash dump inside the stove. Bill wanted to increase the height, but Günter judged that the higher load would be too tippy and too heavy for the horse to pull anyway. Furthermore, the available plastic tarpaulin wouldn't cover the load to keep it dry. Soggy hay would rot. He offered Bill the chance to harness up with the horse. Bill declined.

The cow adapted to its own wagon easily. It must have had earlier experience Emma deduced. The calf followed mother closely without being tied. The smaller wagon too was loaded with as much hay and grain as the animal could pull. If they lifted its tarpaulin on one side, Emma reasoned, and joined it with the similar one on the horse's wagon, it would make a rude shelter in case of wet weather.

The adult goats were tethered to the back of the wagons making it look like they were pushing. The kids followed, complaining a lot, but didn't push much.

With boards from the fallen house, they yoked wheelchairs in pairs – a cross piece on each and long pieces joining the front one to the back. On these platforms they carried the kitchen cupboard loaded with preserves with chicken boxes lashed on top. The boxes had been turned into pens by dowels – straight stems actually - piercing the top and bottom of the open face. In space left, baggage, hardware and utensils they found were tied on with strips of sheeting found around the site. The previous pushers got to move the wagon into which their conveyances had been turned. You could push or pull – those were the options.

There were no trucks to dodge. These roads seemed not to be on their routes. So, the pavement was potholed and deteriorating. The hills were killers. The cow and horse had to be double-yoked and even, so everyone had to help push the big wagons. It usually took four to move one wheelchair wagon up a slope. It wasn't the going up that was the biggest problem. Going down required all their strength to keep things from running away.

Nixie had her own hook to hang from on each wagon depending on where she was riding. Mabel had created a cylinder for her to ride in from one of her parent's quilts. As she hung from her various hooks, she cheered on the efforts of the grownups.

Their progress was glacial. Günter's estimate was hugely over optimistic. There were days when they only made it down into a river valley, across the bridge and up the other side. Rainy days were reluctantly spent in camp, they reasoned, rather than try to dry things out. Even so it stretched out the time and the food they had to the desperation point. One of the young goats became dinner that night; its bones and other parts dried to jerky before they went on.

They followed an inland route that had not been farmed. The hills were not as steep as closer to the lake far in the distance and more forested so there were places to hide if they needed them. If they ran into another bunch of vigilantes, they decided they'd leave everything, baby included, in the roadway and dash for cover. If others came to commandeer what they had, they would use the rifles they had to shoot them down.

One morning after walking all night, they hid along the forested track while Günter went ahead to make a decision about which way to go at the 'T' intersection ahead, next night. He came back with the news. There were no weeds growing in the center of the road, so it had been scraped. It was being tended. He'd found buggy tracks and horse droppings along the crossroad. He recognized them immediately – right axle width, right wheel thickness. Hoof prints showed it was a small horse not a heavy horse that had gone by. The spacing said the horse had been moving briskly. The prints were made yesterday so people travel openly in daytime. They must feel safe.

"Could you tell which way it was travelling?" Bill asked.

Gunter pointed west.

Emma looked hard at Günter. Mabel spotted hope but also something else in the stare. An unspoken question passed between them.

"Yes, it was shod," he replied.

Bill was perplexed. "What does that mean?" he asked.

"Well, our horse, your friend 'General', does not wear horseshoes. His hooves wear off in the dirt and on the gravel roads we've been travelling. But if he had to travel better roads, with paving, he'd need to wear shoes to protect his feet. And to get shoes, he'd need to know a blacksmith or Ferrier about every two months. A blacksmith is the Canadian Tire Store of life now, I think. If a blacksmith doesn't have it, he or she can make it. That buggy was driven by one of our people, I expect. That buggy was driven on roads enough to need shoes. Where that horse went is a community big enough to support a blacksmith."

"... And that community is the one we grew up in," Emma interrupted, but it wasn't as happy, and Mabel had expected. *There was some sort of apprehension under it*, she thought. She might have come from here, but would they find welcome again?

They pulled the wagons together, set up their shelter in case it rained and went to sleep happier than they had in a long time. Mabel only snatched a few hours during the night. Nixie saw to that. She slept swinging in her cocoon and with daylight, she was ready to play. Günter too got up in mid-morning to see if he was right about his deductions.

"I suggest I go ahead on foot to see if I can make contact. Hopefully I can connect with some of them and make plans. I'll be walking in unannounced. Better one of us than all at once. People change, you know. I think I need to see if we still have kin about here."

It was agreed that Günter would set out after another night's rest.

"You might be gone a couple days to find our family," Emma advised. They killed another of the young goats that night so that they all could have good meals for several days. If Günter didn't return by the third day, they would head west. Emma could find their old farm and that is where Günter would meet them.

"Please come back soon," Emma whispered into her husband's ear before he set out next morning.

16

Günter heard the sound of a triangle about midday calling to workers in the field – thrashers – to stop for a meal. How long had it been since he last heard that sound?

He came around the edge of the woodlot so he could see the harvested field. A trestle table was visible halfway down the field in the shade along the fence and a group of men were either at it, or almost so. He carefully climbed the split-rail fence enclosing the harvested space and headed towards the group. He walked slowly forward through the dusty stubble. Was that bread he could smell on the breeze?

From the body language of the women who were looking past the men they were serving and then the turning of the men themselves, it was obvious he had been seen. He held up both hands as he approached. A group of three men, big like himself moved toward him. Günter stopped; the others closed to within three steps. They could talk across the space but neither could reach across it.

"Guten Tag," Günter greeted. He hoped he'd established his membership in the community through his greeting. "I am looking for the Werner family. They used to live around here."

"Wie heißen Sie?" one of the men asked aggressively.

"Günter Werner," Günter replied.

"Woher kommen Sie?"

"A long way away," Günter replied. He looked past the group at the rest of the harvesters. They were all on their feet standing clear of the benches and ready to act, food forgotten on the table.

The leader muttered something to one of the others who immediately strode back to those around the table. The woman he returned with had to be the matriarch – grey haired, tightly tied back, wide shoulders, stalky. She walked to the group leader's elbow. "Who are you looking for?" she demanded.

"I'm looking for any member of the Werner clan." He pronounced the 'W' like a 'V'.

"Why?" she demanded.

"I think they may be relatives. I need a place to stay the winter and I came a long way to find them. There are 5 others with me back down the road – three women and a man … oh, and one infant. We'd be glad to work for our keep."

There was a muttered exchange in which he heard his name mentioned. "We have some animals as well," he interrupted, "and we are carrying feed that will keep some over winter. They need shelter also."

"Tell us exactly how you are related to the Werners," the older woman demanded.

"It is a long story. Before the plague, there was a man named Günter Werner. He owned this farm. He had three children, a daughter and two sons. The children all hated farming and got really good jobs in the city. Nobody wanted the farm except the guy down the road who had a huge chicken operation. He needed a place to dump his manure – really needed it. So, he paid a lot for the farm. The Werners took that money and went away. They were my kinfolk. I came back wondering if any of the grandchildren might have returned here. Or maybe Günter's brothers have children still in the area. We've fallen on hard times and need time to regroup to get started again.

A longer conversation broke out. Nodded heads seemed to validate Günter's details. Those still at the table had moved towards Günter out of curiosity. The details had to be exchanged with them also but out of Günter's hearing. A consensus was finally reached. More information needed to be gathered. It was decided to invite the stranger to eat with them and work the afternoon.

Günter forced himself to eat carefully. He took small portions because he was not sure how well his body would respond to the bounty before him considering he'd been on restricted rations for weeks. Everyone noticed but nobody said anything. With three others, he was sent to scythe down the last corner of the field. Everyone noticed his sweep, the way he stopped to sharpen the blade with a stone that he slipped into his hip pocket with practiced skill. When he joined with the others to stook sheaves, nobody had to show him how to do anything. Everyone agreed, this man had done this before.

"Sleep in the hay mow to-night," he was told. No stranger was going to be invited indoors. Next morning, he appeared at the back door with a pail of milk from one of the cows as one of the children was being sent to deliver his breakfast. The first of the neighbours was arriving to do the threshing.

"Would you like to bring up your family," he was invited.

"If you could send men with a wagon and two extra horses with me, we could make the trip more quickly than I could do alone," Günter responded.

A discussion ensued about sending men to help and how this would delay the gathering of the grain from the field. Everyone agreed the weather would hold so two men and a team could be spared.

After a couple hours on the road, Günter called them to a stop and started singing a German drinking song from an old musical. They proceeded another few minutes, stopped again and again he burst into song.

The men were confused. "My comrades know it is me coming. They will not be hiding," he explained. He didn't say that the women would not open fire either if they heard the song, they had decided would be a code for things being safe.

The fresh team replaced General on the large wagon; General was moved to their host's wagon where he pulled the hand luggage that had been on the wheelchair carts. The cow and her calf walked with the goats behind the wagons. By sunset they were all in the barnyard and neighbours headed home to their own farms.

"It's surprising, you know," said another of his minders as Günter unharnessed the team of which General was a part, "to see someone so young able to manage horses so easily."

Günter shrugged and observed, "they are well trained horses. I just have to follow their lead." The answer surprised the farmer even more. No city-slicker took instructions from a horse.

Emma asked if they could wash their clothes and bathe their smelly bodies. Facilities were quickly provided. The travelers were all cleanly clothed in their spare clothes by bedtime, but they would still be sleeping on clean hay in the barn. They had wet laundry on the top rail of a fence waiting for the sun next day.

They were invited to hang it on the clothesline with clothespins. "It will be windy today. It would be wrong to let clean clothes be blown off the fence into the mud," explained the older woman.

Because of their late arrival, it was not until the next morning that everyone was formally introduced. The older woman, Elizabeth, missed Emma's name in the process of ladling out breakfast porridge for all into bowls. It was not until later that she asked her son, Walter, the one who had done most of the questioning of Günter the day before, what Günter's wife's name was. When he said it, she missed the shelf on which she intended to put the washed-up mug in her hand. It clattered to the counter.

Walter was startled. "What? She said her name was Emma."

The lady, wide-eyed, replied. "My Grandmother's name was Emma, and her husband was named Günter," she whispered.

"Got to be a coincidence," muttered her son. "Anyway, we've got to get that crop in from the field before it gets wet. See how well our guests work out also. See you at lunch."

Walter and Günter spent the morning gathering the stooks of grain from the field and bringing them up to the barn for threshing. The grain was dumped into the granary; the straw was baled and stacked into the other end of the barn from where the hay was piled. It was dusty, dirty work and Günter was more than weary at the end of it. But the crop was in and safe, and there was a deep satisfaction that was equal to the refreshing sluicing of water that took away the grime.

After a day's rest, they were called to work on their neighbour's fields as they had worked on theirs. Günter and Emma were leaning on the fence waiting for Walter to come out. Günter had the horses harnessed. He was rolling his shoulders to try to get the stiffness out. However familiar the task and yesterday's rest, he still had muscles that hadn't done it for a long time.

"You know, as I fell asleep last night," Günter said, "I looked up at those joints up there," he tossed his head towards the barn roof. "We built well in those days didn't we!"

"You can be rightfully proud," Emma agreed as she too thought of how the whole community came together to raise that barn - the one into whose darkness they stared last night - in one day. Every woman in the neighbourhood brought food to share and Emma despite her youth, came bearing the family contributions to the barn-raising.

Günter remembered being told to go to the field to bring in the hay that had dried. They were one of few with the machine to do it. It was a big statement of confidence from his father to let him drive the team out by himself. His father knew that the team knew the job. They'd keep an eye on his young son.

It was no small statement of confidence, in another way, to send a young boy to the field to bring in hay. Quite apart from the mechanics and effort, there was the risk of failed judgement. If the hay was baled damp, it would heat up as it decomposed and could burst into flame. In a few minutes, the years of saving for materials, the hundreds of hours of community effort could go up in smoke along with the winter's security. To send your son to bring baled hay to the barn was a test of all you had taught as a father.

So young Günter drove to the field with the hay rake, past a flat building site littered with hand-hewn beams, already tenoned to fit into the sockets on the posts. You could hardly see the wood for the crowd of men awaiting the instructions of the barn master. By the time Günter returned from rolling the hay to complete the drying, a skeleton of post-and-beam arches marked the place he would store his load later. When he brought the baler back, the roof was on and men were hammering barn boards on all sides. The din was unforgettable. And when he came up the lane with the wagonload of bales, there it stood – bright in the setting sun - a testament to community purpose and time-honoured know-how. No charioteer ever paraded so proudly in front of his audience. To be there that day, was to be in the presence of a miracle. He had to wipe away a tear as he thought of that moment.

"And the well is still sweet," Emma said quietly. Günter looked at his wife that he married more than a hundred years ago and smiled. "I'm going to offer the apples we collected on the way, to make pies," she said. "I think I still remember how."

Walter interrupted with his arrival. "Is your horse up to the job today?" he asked as he took a walk around the animals and checked the harnessing. Again, he was surprised at how professionally the job was done. No loose straps, everything snug but not too tight. He looked at the wagons. All the tools and water jugs they would need were aboard and secure. Bill joined them during the inspection, and they were ready.

"The General didn't complain," Günter said. "Actually, he asked what was taking you so long." Both men laughed and climbed up on their respective wagons, clicked the horses into action and away they went. Günter waved back to Emma. She waved with her free hand as she headed for the kitchen.

"We passed a ruined orchard on our way," Emma said as she called through the screened doorway into the kitchen. "If you have the other ingredients, I could offer them to make pies for the men." She nodded at Irene and Mabel playing with Nixie who was crawling about on the flat surface of the porch floor.

Elizabeth was still wrestling with her son's revelation of their guest's name. She pushed the door wide for Emma to enter with two dozen apples in a sheet sack. "What do you need?" Elizabeth asked. It was a test to see if her guest knew much about kitchen work. She moved the pans of rising bread dough aside to give working space.

By lunch, Elizabeth was thoroughly perplexed. How could someone so young, be so adept. Emma had peeled the apples with a paring knife so quickly, without once breaking the peel. She sliced the apples while carrying on a conversation as if her hands were working by themselves. She advocated making pies with at least three types of apples. "Better flavour," she commented. Elizabeth had never heard of such a subtlety. She asked for spices that most people can't name let alone know what to do with. The running monologue on how to treat the dough mix to make the crust flaky rather than hard, was fascinating. How could so much skill be in someone so young?

Elizabeth continued with her bread-making job, punching down the dough and then cutting it into lumps for the many loaf pans that sat greased and waiting in a row. As she went about her tasks, she was surprised at how easily Emma moved in the kitchen. She didn't need to ask for things. She simply opened the right cupboard door or drawer and there was the bowl or the pie plate. She had the fire roaring in the cook stove. She bounced a spray of water into the oven to test if it was hot enough to bake pies. She flicked dampers open and closed without asking what they would do. The pies were golden brown and once again, without asking, she found the board needed to protect the kitchen table while the pies cooled. They had not boiled over either. Who was this woman?

A pair of delighted squeals came from the verandah. "She's walking," cheered Mabel. "Come see. Nixie just took three steps together." Before leaving the kitchen, Emma checked the fire. The oven was down a little in temperature. She slid the pans of risen dough into the oven without even asking.

Nixie stood wavering, arms widespread, within the circle of women now surrounding her. She'd left the chair against which she had been standing and was focused hard on Mabel's outstretched hands, a couple steps away. She tottered forward one step, another, and one more and tipped into Mabel's hands. Everyone cheered. Nixie smiled in wide-eyed wonder at the reaction.

Emma got up and returned with the leftover pie filling that would not fit into the pie shells, some spoons, some cups, and a pitcher of water. They had finished their snack when they smelled the aroma of fresh bread. Elizabeth realized she'd forgotten to put it in the oven. She scrambled to get up.

"I put them in," Emma explained putting a gentle hand on her arm. "They'll be done in a few minutes."

In the time it took to pick up the cups, count the spoons and finger-wipe the bowl, the bread seemed done. "I'll get these," Emma said collecting the dishes. "You get the bread."

Elizabeth pulled the pans from the oven onto the cleared wooded boards where the pies had been, tapping each with her forefinger for the tell-tale sound of it being properly cooked. When she looked for the pies, she noticed that Emma had already moved them into the special carrier with the adjustable shelves and drop-down door. "That's a very clever carrier," complimented Emma. "I noticed it as we worked and presumed it was what you used to carry pies."

"It's been around here since my mother's day," Elizabeth bragged. "It might have belonged to my grandmother. I don't recall. But it is the perfect size for those plates. You can take out shelves to leave space to carry tall cakes also."

Emma caught herself just in time from saying, *"I know."*

By the time the dishes were washed up, the bread could come out of the pans and the pans could be cleaned.

The day had turned cool but remained bright as the women walked down the lane on their way to the neighbours to add their contributions to the mid-day meal. Everyone was coated up. Elizabeth had her basket of bread and butter; Emma carried the pies by the bale handle of the box. Irene had a container of water in her backpack and metal mugs clattering on a cord looped around the top. Mabel had the baby, now fast asleep, in the child's coat carrier.

"Tell me about yourselves," Elizabeth invited as they set out down the lane. Each waited for the other to start.

"I was a child of the plague years," Irene said. "I can't have children. I've been working in a company in the city."

She had to give the corporate name in response to Elizabeth's query. Details were being collected. She continued. "Mabel's husband was part of the executive suite. She and I fell in together." She had made up the story to avoid explaining where they really came from and when she paused, Mabel picked up her thread.

"I was the trophy wife of a very self-centered money-maker. I got an unlimited bank account and he got to brag how handsome and virile he was. I was replaced by another; the bank account was not. I met Irene on a social platform. I think it was at a coffee shop we noticed Emma and Günter and got to talking with them. They said they were headed this way and we thought we had nothing to lose.

"Günter and I grew up around here – over closer to Benton," Emma said.

"There are a lot of conservative people over there," Elizabeth interjected.

"We left for the big city and found we really didn't belong there. Ever hear of a company called DL Inc.?"

"I don't think so."

"It should remain so. Anyway, we were downsized and thought we might return to our roots. We met Mabel and Irene here. Bill worked at DL and was similarly disenchanted."

"So, Nixie is the child of you and your dead-beat husband, Mabel?" Elizabeth asked pointedly.

"Close enough," Mabel said trying to suggest there might have been a darker affair that she didn't want to talk about. They walked along is silence for a while, the breeze steady and cool from the north.

"How did you come by the livestock?" Elizabeth persisted. If she was going to invite these people to stay any longer than it took to harvest, she needed to know everything about them.

"We rescued them from a farm that was destroyed by a tornado back about a month ago."

"We saw that storm, I think," Elizabeth added. After a week of hot humid weather – went by to the north of us."

"Might be the same," Emma agreed. "We found a bunch of wheelchairs and stuff in the barn that blew down. Who keeps wheelchairs eh? The furniture and preserves we rescued from the wreckage of the house. The apples we found in a damaged shed full of apples and droids who probably harvested them. It would be wrong to leave so much good food to rot or to those who couldn't appreciate it."

"Hmmmm," said Elizabeth.

"Have you lived here long?" Emma finally asked Elizabeth.

"The place belonged to my grandmother I'm told. We came here on visits – Birthdays, that sort of thing, when I was a baby. I don't remember that. We lived in the city then. My grandparents sold out to a factory farm, and I don't know where they went. When my dad died during the plague, Mom decided to get out of the city and looked here. Both her brothers had died also so she was pretty much on her own. The guy who ran the chicken farm needed all the help he could get because his work force mostly died. So, she moved here and got a long lease. The house was still standing and filled with the old furniture. It fixed up well. I don't think she really liked living in the country – it's so isolated, but it was better than being sick. And if she died in the city, what would happen to me? So, we stayed here. There was a community to rely on."

"What was her name?" asked Emma idly.

"Hanna," she replied and then added, "We turn here." Elizabeth directed them onto a path leading into a woodlot. "Watch the footing."

"I married the chicken farmer's son. No surprise there," Elizabeth resumed. "He was pretty much the best catch available, and we had Walter right away. That really re-hooked me up with the local German culture that I think my grandmother grew up in."

"My husband and his Dad died in a barn fire that wiped out the chicken business so it left Mom, Walter, and I pretty much on our own – well except for the neighbours. It was a huge support to be part of a group like that." The sky brightened as they reached the edge of the woods, and they could see the farmhouse and barn ahead.

"Walter married a local girl, but she ran off to the city maybe five years ago. Mom died shortly after. Walter hasn't expressed any interest in other women since."

Mabel caught the last comment like a fly ball. *Hmmmm*, she thought.

They all directed their attention to the house and barn they were approaching. "We'll be setting up in the barn I suspect," Elizabeth suggested. "It will be out of the wind and space will be cleared ready for the hay they'll be bringing in later."

*

"I think we'll be doing his second cut of hay or baling what he cut himself. Hope he cut it. Be a shame to waste the dry weather. It can't last much longer," Walter said after they reined in at the entrance to the neighbour's laneway.

"Do I smell smoke?" Günter asked. He knew as soon as he smelled it that the steam-powered thrashing machine would be chuffing away just over the hill waiting to be fed. They crested the rise, and it was as Günter had guessed. Earlier neighbours were already in the field loading armloads of grain stalks onto wagons. The rattle of the thresher as it separated the wheat grains from the cascade of straw pouring out the other end told everyone that the adjustments were done and to hurry with the next loads.

"We got enough help with the grain," the neighbour explained. "Can you cut the rest of the hay?" the neighbour asked when they stopped in the yard. He explained that he had cut only part of his field.

Günter looked at Walter. "I saw that as we came up the lane. I can start with the scythe. If you get the rake," he nodded to the implement beside the barn, "and turn what he did, that should give us enough to bale after lunch."

Walter was a bit surprised at the authority in Günter's voice as he directed more than suggested what was obviously the best way to use their skills and manpower.

"Güt," the neighbour replied, and everyone fell to his tasks. Bill really felt like a fifth wheel on the wagon. He could lift and move whatever others told him to, but he had no skill to anything else in field work. His attention was really caught by the woodlots they passed on the way. He'd asked Walter who they belonged to and resolved to meet those men, if he could, to ask if he could assess the lots for timber that should be cut to let the rest grow. So, he spent his day describing his skill to as many as he could, saying that he could help them manage those woodlots and give them the resources they needed to improve their farms. He got an attentive hearing from all to whom he spoke.

It was as they were shaking hands with the other workers before heading home to evening meals that one of the men held Günter's hand longer than necessary. "I think I know that horse," he said. "How came you by it?"

"It is distinctive with that blaze on its chest," Günter agreed. "You've heard that we came from the city. As we passed a farm that was wrecked by a windstorm, we heard animal sounds from the barn. The house was flattened – just a pile of splintered lumber. Nobody was around. The barn was badly pushed over - would have collapsed had not the hay inside held it up. But the door from the stables below was jammed so the animals would have starved or died without water had we not happened by. We forced a way through to get the animals out." The men looked at each other. "You say it looks like one you know," Günter said.

"It looks a lot like the one I sent off with my son and his wife. They wanted to grow apples a little closer to the lake up north. He got an orchard started and producing and then came back to get married. They left about three years ago. We haven't heard from them since."

Günter looked sadly at the man who was just then, joined by a stout woman. "Come along Herman. Cows have to be milked."

Abruptly, Günter shook his head as though confused. "Can we talk about this maybe another day? There are a lot of reasons why the horse you gave your son might wind up on another person's farm in three years, if this one is it. Could we get you to come by the Werner place on a rainy day or when you can? That's where we're staying until we figure out what we can do."

Herman nodded and responded to the hustling of his wife; Günter turned to see Bill and his own women were all sitting on the wagon waiting for him. Everyone was looking for a ride home instead of walking.

*

"I've invited Herman to come over when he can to talk about my horse," Günter explained to Walter. Anyone attentive to weather could feel the approach of rain.

"I hope the last hay we cut was taken in," Walter replied.

"I just wanted to be sure it was OK to ask him to come by. We don't know the protocols."

"It's OK," Walter said.

"I also wanted to build a pen for the goats on the south side of the barn," he pointed to the area. "It would be a lean-to roof. I'd like to bale up the hay we brought with your machine and then use the bales to enclose the space to protect the animals. That is if you'll let us stay." There was no response as both looked at the space to be occupied.

"I noticed your fields are really clean. You've done great weed control. That hay we brought probably isn't as clean and the manure from the animals will contaminate your fields if it is spread there. I was trying to think of a way to keep the weeds in one place where the goats could look after them."

"They'll eat the walls," Walter observed. The most important question seemed to be the animals' welfare.

"I won't make it easy. I thought I could put up a temporary fence inside to keep them from eating themselves out of house and home."

Walter smiled at the phrase and the thought and nodded.

"We need to talk about saying here till Spring," Günter continued. "We could build an enclosure for ourselves out of the bales in the barn too. It would be cramped but warm enough for the winter. We don't want to be a trouble – well… more than we can help."

"You couldn't have a fire or lamp."

"Well, I didn't say it would be easy, but we can't be on the road under canvas especially with the child."

"We should talk. Let me speak to my mom."

*

"Günter asked Walter to confirm the invitation to Herman and his wife to come over," Emma said to Mabel and Irene. They were all scrubbing up clothes and diapers on borrowed washboards, hoping to get them dry before the rain came. "The weather will turn by tomorrow," Emma had cautioned. Bill and Günter had gone to the woodlot to cut poles for a shelter for the goats. "Herman thinks General is the horse he gave his son and bride when they moved back up north to an apple farm the young man had created."

The announcement fell like an anvil. Mabel set to scrubbing a diaper with renewed vigour. "We'll have to show them the other things we recovered from the house. Maybe they'll confirm that it was their son and daughter-in-law we buried."

"Why did he have to say we found the horse at a farm? Why didn't he say we found it on the road, running loose," exploded Mabel.

"I guess it's about integrity," Emma said. "Imagine a parent seeing his child move off full of hope and worrying every day about how they made out. When we show up with his horse, they can't help but think the worst. We…"

"I am thinking exactly that," shouted Mabel as she slammed the cloth against the board and ran off crying uncontrollably.

*

Günter and Emma had talked long into the night. "It isn't our house anymore. We sold it," Emma insisted. "All we can ask is if they will let us stay. It is wrong to drift up to the door and say we're your grandparents, so we'd like the master bedroom."

"We could ask to build another house maybe next spring. We could cut wood over the winter for it. Maybe we could ask to lease a plot."

"We thought we would be able to help our children in their senior years and all we are is an unexpected burden they don't even know about. This sure hasn't worked out as we thought it would."

"I guess we should try to clear the air tomorrow."

Emma squeezed his hand in reply.

There was an awkward silence after Günter asked the question next morning after breakfast. The animals had been milked as usual but with the rain, there would be no fieldwork to-day. Inside repair to stalls would keep Walter busy.

"I'm building a wattle fence inside the hay wall to keep the goats from eating it," Bill announced as soon as he put down his spoon. He stood, took his empty porridge bowl to the sink, and left. Irene, Mabel, and Nixie quickly excused themselves to visit the animals.

"You are good folk," Elizabeth said finally with reservation. "You told me openly where you came from and how you got here, but I need to hear more." It was as close to saying she didn't believe Emma as civil conversation allowed.

Emma looked at Günter, who nodded. *Here goes*, she thought.

"You're right, Elizabeth. I could feel you watching me in the kitchen. I do things too fast."

"And Günter works in the field like no city-slicker I ever saw," Walter interrupted. "You're too young to know how to do that stuff. You said you came from around here but you're going to need to elaborate on that a bit more."

"OK," Emma said and took a big breath. "Günter and I did grow up here." She tried to leave the feeling that she meant in the neighbourhood rather than in this house in particular. "We sold our farm when we got too old, and the children had no interest in farming. We couldn't abide the life in the Retirement Home anymore. It was so formal, trivial – I don't know. We just felt we were killing time. And we knew nobody there. The things they did were petty and infantile. With all the money from the sale of the farm, we thought of trying to set up some sort of endowment or charity thing. It was more trouble than we imagined." Only the hiss of the rain on the roof filled the space when Emma stopped.

"At about that time we heard about a company that offered to bring you back in the future with the body you had as a young adult. It was like buying back time. You'd still have all the memories and skills of your earlier life. We thought about it a long time and then decided to do it. We committed to finding our children or grandchildren when we came back and look after them as they had so generously looked after us when we were so old."

"So back in the spring, we were resurrected. Please don't get too caught up on that word – just say we woke up in a bed and it was fifty years after we went to sleep, and we had the bodies you see. I can tell you more details than you want to hear later but as soon as we could, Günter and I set out to return to our roots. Bill, Irene, and Mabel joined us for their own reasons. One other didn't come at the last minute."

"And that brings us to this moment. I don't know how to say this any other way. I believe, we are your grandparents."

Stunned silence.

Emma hurried on in spite of the incredulous faces, verging on scorn, looking at her. "The reason I work so well in this kitchen is because I did so for fifty years — often with you as an infant when you came to visit from the city." She looked hard at Elizabeth. "You haven't changed things much. It was a pie recipe that I found as a bride that I used for the thrashers the other day. I'm glad it survived the test of time. Günter made the pie carrier we used that day. I can't count the pies I've put in it. Unless I'm mistaken the leaves to extend this table are behind that door." Emma he nodded to the doorway to the Parlour. "I'll bet you still have the crocheted doilies I made with your mother and which you chewed on as an infant, in the back of the top drawer of the dining cabinet over there."

Günter jumped in to add his two cents worth. "I wonder if your handprint is still in the stable floor beside the door. I pushed your little hand into the fresh cement the day your dad and your uncles helped me pour it. I can tell you the last places in the back field to dry out after a wet spring."

He sort of ran out of gas at that point and waved away the minutiae he thought he would offer as proof that they were who they said they were. For Elizabeth's part, every detail was a proof that could only come from someone there at the time. Yes, her handprint was in the cement with her name and her uncle's, as well as her Grandpa Günter's. Yes, the doilies and table leaves were exactly where Emma said they were. But it strained credibility that these young faces could be those of her own grandparents who had been gone half a century and were wrinkled and bent when she last remembered them.

Emma had picked up the story. "Well, we expected to come back to help our children and grandchildren as they so often helped us. We arrived too late for the former; we hope to stay and be to you what you were to us. And that is why we're here and we'd like to stay but to do so we need more of the help you offered back then before we can help you in the next years you have left."

"Can you see the future?" Elizabeth asked, next to tears.

"No, we can't," Emma replied. "We're just really good on the distant past. We can talk your ear off about what happened back when."

"We need to figure out where you'll stay," Walter said into the silence that followed. The decision was made. "You can't stay in the barn."

"I think we can," Emma said. "It won't be the first time and we know a lot more now than we did then."

"You're just looking for a roll in the hay," chided Günter. "Remember what happened last time?"

"Yes, I do," Emma answered dreamily, and then hurriedly added, "but maybe Mabel and the baby would be better inside when it gets cold."

"Let's talk about that while we fix those stalls," Günter suggested.

17

Mabel was uncertain why Nixie took to her as she did. Emma had suggested it might have been her blond hair and blue eyes. The smashed body they buried had long blond hair. There was no way to tell the eye colour.

In any of the moments when they passed Nixie about, it was Mabel to whom she eventually held out her arms for rescue. Safely in Mabel's arms, the child would turn confidently to look at anything else – not so with the others.

"She's imprinted on you," Emma had said after the first few days – as though that explained anything. Emma then had to recount what happened if you were the first thing that goslings saw after they hatched from their eggs. She told them all about the flock of geese that followed her around when she was a child because she picked them up before they saw their mother.

Over the rest of their trek, Nixie was never out of reach whether she was in the carrier, Mabel made for her or hanging safely out of the way on the wagon they all were pushing. Mabel found she could not even think of eating before the baby was fed. She had no compunction at all about calling a halt so she could change the baby's diaper. Mabel became a mother bear!

It was when the child's presence needed to be explained during their walk to the neighbour's that Mabel began to feel a deep terror, she could not name. She thought it had all passed until Günter invited the neighbour's to come to talk about the horse. Damn his virtuous ethics. There was no doubt in Mabel's mind that Nixie was the neighbour's grandchild. She could not bear that thought that someone who only offered a possible blood link might take this child who could have died without the attention she had given.

So, while Emma and Günter said they would try to explain things to Elizabeth and Walter, she had to get out of the room. The thought that they might be staying indefinitely next door to a couple who might descend at any time and claim the child as theirs was too much to dwell on.

Mabel had scooped up the baby in her carrier as they left for the barn. Irene, Mabel, and Nixie spent all morning patting the goats, talking to the cows and horses, feeding the chickens, trying to keep Nixie from putting everything she picked up in her mouth. Every animal gave her a lick. *There must be something tasty about drooly babies*, Mabel thought.

Irene was mostly a silent and supportive presence in these situations. She knew intuitively of Mabel's anxiety. She did not harangue Mabel with obvious questions. She just lent her quiet but strong closeness to her friend who felt so storm-tossed.

And then, rather than get back to the kitchen in the midst of things she could not control, Mabel stuffed Nixie in her carrier and hoisted onto her back for a walk down the lane and back through the woods - rain notwithstanding. Irene, sensing she was not wanted, returned to the house. *Surely, they've come to some decision by now*, Irene thought.

Nixie gabbled in Mabel's ear about all the wonderful things an infant can see over an elder's shoulder and then found the collar of Mabel's coat. She chewed on it until she fell asleep.

*

Herman and his wife Anna came over in their buggy after three days of rain. That he unhitched the horse at Walter's suggestion and tied it in shelter beside the hay wagon in the barn said the invitation would be longer than a church service. They met around the kitchen table rather than in the parlour because it was the largest room in the house. Despite the weather, Bill made himself scarce. He went off to talk to neighbours about their woodlots and to assess the wood in them.

Emma and Günter fell right into the conversational protocols with gentle questions about the crops, the animals, preserves – the small talk of close friends. Irene leaned forward to listen but contributed little. Elizabeth had found a box of wooden children's toys for Nixie to play with. Mabel snatched at the chance to get out of the room to try them out. Secretly, Mabel had wondered if she could run off with the child if Anna and Herman decided that the child must be their grandchild. She had the money and diamonds she had kept hidden. Could she get to town – wherever that was, and use her wealth to build them a life? The absurdity of the plan was discouraging. She picked up the baby and headed down the hallway, ostensibly to change a diaper, as she heard Emma start to talk about one of her recipes.

Emma shared her recipe for apple pie with Anna claiming it came from quite a while ago. Elizabeth had decided that nobody else needed to know that the young couple they had befriended were, in fact, her grandparents. It would raise a lot of questions that would be hard to answer and might even have religious significance that would more likely divide than bind, for others. Let the newcomers be known as refugees with distant roots to the place and leave it at that.

But eventually the horse and its origin came up. It was why everyone was meeting after all. Günter conceded that it might, in fact, be the horse that Walter had sent off with his son, but maybe there were other pieces of this puzzle they could connect. Was the horse found in the remains of the son's farm or had the young man sold it to someone else?

"We found other things amidst the wreckage of the house," Emma said. "There were two bodies, a man and woman – both young but they were not recognizable. The wall had fallen on them. The best we could do is give them a Christian burial and we did, but we found nothing that could tell us their names." The news was met with grim silence.

"We recovered some kitchen things. I don't know if you'd recognize any of them." She lifted a small wooden crate of items onto the table.

There is something soul saddening about a collection of worn kitchen utensils. They are the symbols of daily sustenance to people unknown. Every day they met someone's needs. These are the intimate reflections of daily life. It is almost embarrassing to be faced with such a collection.

So, it as with the parade of items that now emerged from a wooden crate for everyone else to see. The metal mug was dinted, the ladles were tarnished and grimy, the knife blade was worn into a curve but still keenly sharp. There were several metal plates, a nesting set of cast iron pots with lids, a kettle that was smashed flat.

"We thought the kettle might be recovered if we could find some tools and an anvil," Emma explained.

Anna nodded and reached for the last item in the bottom of the box. It was a meat grinder – like a thousand others in their neighbourhood. Tough meat cuts found their way through those things to become hamburger and sausage. With the proper blades, purees for infants or sauces for adults were possible. They never wore out. The worst calamity was the loss of the different blades that came with them. With care, a bride who had one as part of her trousseau could count on passing it on to her children.

"It's hardly worn," Anna observed as she lifted if out.

"I looked for the accessory blades," Emma said. "I could find three."

"The other one is in the machine," Anna observed. "They are all there." She studied the wooden handle, lightly stained by use, and instinctively grasped the handle to judge the fit. Her fingertips found a roughness on the underside, and she rolled the rough space up and tilted it to the light.

Emma saw Anna tighten; eyes squint close as tears rolled down her cheek. Emma took the tool from her as Anna slumped back into her chair. In the wooden handle was delicately carved a name so that it would not be lost at a bee where many women would be working together. "Julia" it said. It was Anna's daughter-in-law's name.

"Oh, I'm so sorry, Anna," Emma said as she leaned toward the stricken mother. Elizabeth, at her side, put a comforting arm around her shoulder. The men sighed and stared at the table, alone in their grief.

Only the patter of raindrops accompanied Anna's soft weeping. She eventually caught her breath and asked in a broken voice. "Do you suppose you could find that farm again, Günter?" she asked. It was the first time anyone had called him by his name.

"I think I could, but it would take a couple days to go each way," he said.

"We'd need to go as a group, he added. "It isn't always safe to travel alone. We had a bad experience."

Herman nodded.

Nixie's cheerful laughter danced down the hall from the room where she was playing with Mabel.

"You should take these things with you, then," Emma said as she placed them back in the crate.

Anna and Herman looked at each other. Everyone around the table knew instinctively that there was another issue to deal with.

"It won't be long before it gets out," Anna said. "Herman's health has taken a step down lately. We doubt we'll be able to keep going on the farm by next seeding time. We need to start re-ordering our lives." She heaved a sigh. "We know that the baby must be Julia's."

Irene heard the pronouncement like a hammer blow.

"Look at the hair, the curls," Anna continued. "Just like Herman's when he was young." She looked at his bald head now. "It would be within our rights to take the child away, but knowing what we do about Herman's health, it would not be in the child's interest. She needs a mother more than a grasping grandmother." She took another shuddering breath and waited to regain her composure.

"Could we all agree that Nixie really is Mabel's child? Do you suppose we could come and visit from time to time – maybe ask your help as we need it? Maybe we could see Nixie as well." Herman looked down in silence. Emma met everyone's eyes around the table.

"It would be best if Nixie stayed with Mabel. We could come and pretend she was ours. Do you think Mabel would let us come and do that? Or could she and Nixie come and live at our house? They could have my son's old room and Mabel could help me with Herman."

"I'll get her," Irene said, jumping at the chance to be useful.

Elizabeth rose at the same time. "It is time for supper. Could you break bread with us rather than ride home in the rain?" There was no protest in the heartbeat where it would have been seemly to protest. "Herman, would you get a leaf for the table behind the parlour room door? I can make some corn meal to go with the bean casserole," she said.

"Let me lay the table," Anna said and quickly moved to the drawer where her back was to the room, and she could wipe away more tears.

Irene returned with Mabel to the kitchen presently both with tear-stained faces. Nixie followed, slapping her hands loudly on the hardwood as she crawled to catch up. Wordlessly, Anna and Mabel embraced. Herman accepted his hug stiffly.

18

"How do you get things you need to buy?" Günter asked Walter. "In days back when, we went in to Benton and got them through the General Store most of the time - things like seed or special spices, fabrics, tools - that sort of stuff. It was rare to go to London."

"We still go to Benton, but we order things from the terminal there. It comes a couple days later. So, you need to make two trips. It better be worth it."

"How do you pay for things?"

"Well, we sell some of our excess produce – vegetables mostly, in the summer, and your account is credited. you never see any cash. Against that money, you can make purchases. We don't pay interest as a matter of policy and conviction. If we don't have the credit on hand, we don't buy it."

"Is there any way to get credit to start out, or expand?"

"Well, the answer is yes if you want to sell your soul to the company store. The interest rates are usurious - in our estimation."

Mabel had been listening to the conversation as she played with Nixie. "Are there any jewelry dealers you know about?" she asked.

"We don't agree with personal adornment," Walter said. "But just so we know where evil lies, I know there are two or three in London. Why do you ask?"

"In a distant day," Mabel answered, "people bought jewelry for special occasions like weddings or special birthdays. I just wondered if people still did that."

"Not in our community. Amongst the ultra-rich there may be some people who do. I just never met anyone who could afford to do that quite apart from why they would." Mabel could see it was not a topic she could pursue.

"I mean what can you do with such things? Eat them? Try to outdo the Lord's blessings you have? Make others envious or greedy? Such things confuse me," Walter admitted.

Topic closed! But Mabel stored the information for another day.

*

With the question of a place to stay resolved and her role as caregiver to a child solidified, Mabel turned to the other security she had concealed from everyone for months – the cache of gold coins and diamonds she'd worn against her skin. In a far distant day, she'd accumulated this horde as insurance against being kidnapped. She'd figured she might be able to use the valuables to pay a ransom. Now she wondered what to do with it. It hadn't brought the security she expected.

The quilted sheet of coins had been tied to her bra, so it hung over her midriff. It was sweat-stained, smelly and weighty. Mabel re-sewed the ties so that she could lift the corners to knot the tiny quilt into a bag. Into the bag, she added the cloth tubes of diamonds, and tied the sac closed. All told, the value had been a little over a hundred thousand dollars back in her earlier days. Today, she wondered if her treasure had any value at all.

She'd given a coin to their benefactors back at the DL site. Did it wind up as jewelry? – pretty baubles about which to chat – no more valuable than glass beads.

From her conversations with their new community members, it seemed that the banking system was completely controlled. If there was a black market through which to sell the coins or diamonds, she had no idea how to access it. Was there a way to get the credit, if the coins or stones had any value at all, into an account they could use to improve the farm? She'd have to find that help beyond this community, if it was worth the trouble. How would she get the help needed to make such a conversion, presuming it was possible, without admitting that she'd been hiding this treasure all along? Sounded sticky - maybe even irrelevant.

She thought of Harold back wherever. He'd have been able to figure out how to create the files or whatever. Maybe Dodger would have been the better choice. She wondered if there would be any way to reconnect with them? What had happened to emails and social media? Would it be worth trying to connect to a world of self-centred indulgence held in place in a symphony of manipulated behaviour?

She had thought about picking out the threads that formed the coin pockets and then abandoned the thought. What for? The pieces would still be as golden, the clink as she bounced them in her hand, would still be as heavy. The crystal gravel would look very unimpressive spread out on a dirty, stained piece of fabric. Tie it up in a bundle and tuck it in her drawer – a tribute to another life. Would she tidy up her thoughts in the same way.

She lay back on the bed, with the baby napping beside her. Six months ago, she had wakened up in a sterile suite from a half-century sleep, tricked into that state by her own complacency and ill intent. The anger she felt at discovering the deception tried to bubble up and then fell back into … nothing. She could hardly recognize herself anymore from the person she now thought she must have been. She remembered the sense of entitlement. She remembered the perfectly laid out plans to tour the world on her husband's money seeking out those of similar affluence. She imagined the offhanded waving away of the price of anything. She would have had anything she wanted as her right.

Now she and Nixie had moved in with Anna and Herman. Talk about a blended family! When Anna had asked her to come and help with her husband, it seemed like an ideal solution for everyone. The child was secure, her grandparents had the youthful help they needed but had lost. She had a new life, whether she liked it or not. And it gave her a space of her own away from male attention. At the Werner's she'd become aware of Walter's growing attention. It had not been unwelcome but here living next door, she had space to consider. Being in the same house could create a situation ... well she just wanted to plan her life rather than have it happen. George had taught her that lesson well enough.

And here she lay absorbed into a community of survivors not because she could buy her way in but because they opened their arms to them in their destitution. Well maybe Günter and Emma proving they were really Elizabeth's relatives was a bigger part. You really didn't throw out your grandparents no matter how they looked. That caused another chuckle. In her old life, she was prepared to murder her husband. What did that say about her?

Harold had raised a question months ago. He wondered if being downloaded into a quantum computer had affected them fundamentally in the way they really saw the world. He said that qubits had three states, not two. Had the third alternative been stamped on them in the process of delinking and relinking? What happened to resolutions that used to be black and white, zero or one? Were they gone? Was everything now a shade of grey? It sure seemed to make life easier to get along in, if confusing. Was that bad? Well, look at her! Where was she now?

"Humph," she said to the room. "This is good enough. Good enough is good enough!"

Moving in with Anna was a step up from camping but only deepened her awareness of the amount she did not know about how to do anything. She had arrived in time to assist with the preserving of a year's supply of garden produce. In her previous life, she simply ordered something. Here she was learning how to do what she had earlier assumed.

Carrots, onions, potatoes, beets, turnips, cabbages, tomatoes, beans, ... the list never ended. And digging them up, cleaning them and then storing them for the winter happened around milking, feeding, and cleaning up after animals. When Mabel didn't have Nixie to entertain in the garden, the child had to be with Grandma ministering to Grandpa's needs. His breathing was shallow and panting like George's and the man could do no manual work at all.

In the evenings there were domestic skills to learn - sewing, knitting, crocheting. Mabel was into the crash course in life skills she had never needed. Once harvest had been completed, things settled a bit and people created reasons to visit each other. With time available, Mabel and Nixie spent time with the Werners and the extended community at socials. So it was, Mabel was swept into the celebrations for Christmas.

Making purchases at the depot in Benton was part of that process. Herman's account had to be accessed for material to make clothes. The ones that Mabel had come with were fifty years out of date but worse, were meant for idle fashion plates in climate controlled mansions rather than working women in unheated or modestly heated rooms. The stuff just didn't stand up.

At the depot where they entered their orders, Anna had cause to appreciate Mabel's skill with the interface. Mabel's red scarf that changed colour when it was twisted, was so admired by Anna. Mabel set out to see if she could get one for her. When the chance arose, Mabel punched in her identification from DL Inc. She was stunned when it worked. Apparently, the machine did not recognize the fact that she had not ordered meals for months.

Mabel started with the way she had gotten her scarf - as a medical device. She increased the size and weight criteria to create a wrap. Details of colour, weave and thermal insulating index had to be entered. It took a long time but when it finally appeared, it looked great on the screen. She wondered if she could access her allowance as well and amazingly enough, the machine charged the cost to her. Quickly Mabel saved here creation in a coded file. When she typed in the delivery address, the computer choked.

"Address not recognized," declared the statement on the screen.

Anna returned from chatting with others to find Mabel pounding the wall beside the uncooperative device. They were walking out to where the buggy waited when Mabel stopped in mid-stride.

"Back in a few minutes," she mumbled to Anna and dashed back to an empty terminal in the Emporium.

Quickly she opened her account and tapped in "Roger the Dodger" and his code that she recalled. The screen glowed steadily then blinked.

"Who's calling?"

"Mabel Twilling." Her code would already be at the top of his screen if it was him, he was talking to. There was another pause.

"What's my middle name?"

Mabel immediately smiled. She'd test him as well. "It isn't Spanish," she typed.

"So, what is my middle name," the screen repeated.

"Brooklyn," she typed.

"Good to hear from you," came the message. "I left a tell-tale to contact me when or if you ever reappeared. Good to hear from you."

"Could you send a special order," and she typed in the code for her saved file, "to this address?"

"Of course - two days."

"Could you establish a secure link with me?" There was a long enough pause to make Mabel wonder if she'd lost the connection when new words appeared.

"Order will arrive with messenger in three days. Harold sends greetings."

"How will I know messenger is secure?"

"Remember how Harold identified Cameron?"

Mabel looked to the ceiling as she searched her memory of the day they had stood wondering if special bots were assigned to special people. In her head she heard what Harold had done. "Y," she typed.

Her screen went blank.

All the way home Mabel was chuckling to herself until Anna demanded she tell what was so funny. "We have to come back in three days," Mabel said.

Anna replied with a list of other priorities which Mabel acknowledged silently.
"Maybe I can get Günter or Emma to bring me in."

Emma said she would be pleased to drive her in. She was looking for an excuse to get away from her granddaughter anyway. *Too many cooks in the kitchen*, was the way she thought about it.

Knowing Mabel had no ability to manage a horse and carriage, Emma jumped at the chance, but it was raining coldly on the third day. Emma wasn't about to abuse the horse with an all-day rain, so it was two days later before they made it to the Benton Emporium to look for Mabel's package.

Before they set out, Mabel asked Emma to bring the account code for Walter's farm account. "You might need it," she replied to Emma's question. "Just trust me."

Emma returned with the information, and they set off. "You may have to pay a surcharge for storage when you didn't pick it up on time, but I wasn't about to make General sick or slip for whatever the store has delivered," Emma justified as they approached their destination.

The Benton Emporium's sign was a local joke. The font size had to be reduced to fit on the storefront. It was just a service desk and a string of computer terminals that marched into the depths of the store. There was a storage room parallel to the terminals accessed by a door behind the desk. The locals had seen that this utilitarian box of a store was crowded into a back corner appropriate to the underwhelming shopping experience it represented. To add to its humilification the Business Improvement Area had decorated signboards around it with photographs of elegant facades and aisles of merchandise from much earlier times.

The rest of the square around which all the displaced business that once thrived there, still stood, had been glassed over. Trees grew in park spaces old storefronts now were open to a climate-controlled street to offering a dizzying variety of places to snack, drink, gossip and share everything else. The Emporium occupied a corner of the place like an abandoned church. Once you picked up whatever you had ordered, you took it to a table to look at it and display for others. If it was the wrong size, colour, whatever, there was someone at hand who could fix it or modify it to make it what you really wanted, and they did it while you waited. It kept the independence skills alive that the on-line industry was determined to stamp out. Mabel was reminded of the hours it had taken to get the computer to make her a scarf she wanted.

"No package for that name," the person on the desk said when they arrived to claim Mabel's purchase, but as she had spoken her name, a bot had mummed into action at the end of the counter and purred out of the white square marked on the floor for such equipment. It approached and scanned her. It looked much like the Cameronbots that had ministered to them back a DL Inc. but his one had a recessed drawer below its screen.

Mabel was surprised when the machine addressed her. "Delivery for Mabel Twilling," it said.

Mabel turned to study the cylinder on wheels. The smooth dome was noticeably deformed with a single dint. "Come this way," Mabel directed and walked to a comfortable table away from others that were occupied. It followed her obediently.

"State security code," the machine stated when they were away from the rest of the line-up.

"Ketchup smear," said Mabel.

The slot below the screen opened and out slid a paper package the size of a folded blanket. She handed the package to Emma. Below the package was a keyboard. Mabel commanded the machine to move closer to shield the screen from the rest of the square.

Mabel typed in her code and Roger's. A reply appeared quickly.

"Hi."

"E, G, B, & I, send greetings," Mabel typed.

"Good news." the screen said.

"Thanks for the parcel."
"Welcome."

"Are these of value? How much?" Mabel held up to the screen in one hand, one of the gold coins she had carried for so long, and one diamond in the other. She turned the coin over and turned the stone. Emma who had been looking around the square for anyone she might know, turned to see what occupied Mabel.

"What are those?" she asked in surprise. Mabel ignored the question, focusing on the droid.

"Closer," the screen dictated. A new sound came from the droid and Mabel thought her hands felt prickly.

"Y & Lots," responded the screen.

"Can you assign value of one," Mabel held up the coin, "to this account," and she rhymed off Anna's farm account." There was a pause.

"For a commission."

"Done."

And this," she held up the diamond, "to …," Mabel turned to Emma, "State the farm's account number."

Emma was a bit startled but eventually typed out the correct sequence from the scrap she pulled from her pocket.

"Insert items," the machine directed.

Mabel placed the coin and diamond on the tray beside the keyboard and they disappeared inside.

"Complete," the machine flashed after a few moments. The tray with the keyboard reappeared but the coin and diamond were gone.

"Can you show both account balances?" Mabel typed.

Emma's hand shot to her mouth when she saw the balances. "That will cover the farm expenses for the year," she gasped.

"And that is after commission. I won't ask what he skimmed off. Would it build you a house?"

"I couldn't live in one that big."

"More?" asked the screen.

"Why value so high?" Mabel inquired.

"Limited supply, few/no workers. More?" the screen repeated.

"Y" And then Mabel asked, "How do we keep contact?"

"Droid will return to your site and wait. It is mine."

"Always the same droid?"

"Y."

"THX," Mabel typed and then asked, "Are spending accounts for I, G, B and E still active?"

"For a fee."

"Do it. Debit my account. Show final balance."

"Get a coffee," the machine directed.

"I think it means this will take a while," Mabel interpreted. Emma wandered off to get them something and visit people she thought she knew. "I might have known that woman's kin," she said. "I think I'll ask her."

"Compatibility adjustments needed," came the eventual reply as they drained their cups. "You are recorded as residing in DL suites in Detroit and travelling. Accounts active. I set up code to route purchases through distant sites but deliveries to you at your site."

"???" typed Mabel.

"Big Brother."

"Suggest concealing items then, as well, to comply with legend you created."

"Already done. Who are you talking to??? Fee charged."

"Give final balance." Mabel did the arithmetic. "Well what good is a hacker if he isn't really good. And do the really good ones come cheap? Who cares? Not my money," she commented to Emma as she logged off. She patted the droid on its dented dome. "We're done," she said.

The droid hummed into motion and departed smoothly through a door beside the service counter into the rear of the building.

"Well, it looks like Roger is doing all right if he has his own droid." Mabel commented on their way to the carriage. "If he does for others what he did for me, he probably owns a fleet of them."

"Where did you get those things?" Emma asked again, finally getting coherent thought back.

"Tell you on the way home. Still got my package?"

Emma held it up.

*

"Old tech," Irene said, based on her repair training, when they described the droid and the experience. "It's why you have to enter your order by keyboard, but it can still talk to you. The talking function has always been a problem not worth the time to fix. But they likely have biometric scanners. That is why the droid responded to your question and came to you. It likely was programmed to recognize your voice and then other details as part of a sequence of verifications. Your code words were the last step in the process. We used to make up passwords of letters and numbers as I recall. This is the same thing but with other details that are harder to hack - I presume."

"You know," she continued, "what I see is the evidence of the severity of the plague. This community endures because they had pioneer skills from way back. The dented droid is there because there aren't enough people to repair things. Centuries of technical advances have disappeared. Mind you the pursuit of that stuff is what laid waste to the world in the first place and who knows how far the weather slide will go?

Bill butted in with his information. "When I delinked, many of the trees I now see in these woodlots simply couldn't grow this far north. Now I find dozens of examples of Carolinian forest species that were only along the north shore of Lake Erie. They died if they came to Toronto. Not now."

"And I was able to access my DL account to buy a gift. It seems Roger saw that mine was open just in case I called. I asked him to see yours are active now as well," Mabel said to the circle around the table at the Werner's.

"I wonder if we'd attract unwanted attention by all of us accessing them from an off-site terminal?" Irene asked.

"Roger has already attended to that." Mabel explained the details.

"Emma had been quiet through the whole conversation but now spoke up. "Do you have any reservations about reconnecting with the DL world? I do. I thought we had escaped that place of synthetic values and greed. Just when I feel I've found roots I can settle with and I'm actually beginning to feel at home, these ghosts from my past threaten to suck me back into their world. I really want nothing more to do with it."

"I don't know if logic is any help in an emotional situation," Irene commented into the silence following Emma's declaration. "Probably not, but here's what I can offer for the less distressing moments that will come later and hopefully before you make a final decision. Like it or not, you have a reservoir of resources at DL Inc. They have contracted to pay them to you as they said they would when you delinked. What you do with them is the issue."

Emma was still twisting her hands in her lap. Irene took her silence as permission to continue. "So, you could decide to buy solar cells or windmills for every place in the community instead of trips or trinkets, if you chose. From what I see and hear, there isn't any religious reason against it, or any woman around who wouldn't bless you for providing running water and LED lights. The funds are waiting for you to use. In your earlier life, you didn't have to think about money. Now it has become a duty for you to manage - if you chose to take it up.

"But where does that end?" Emma complained. "Why not buy the frills that come with that life - the droids, the automatic equipment that does everything? I could lead the life of a bored bystander waiting to be served. How does anyone with wealth avoid sliding into that world of entitlement and dissolution?"

"Well, you can choose and I'm sure the local hair-splitters could advise anyone who asks or not. As for me, I'm planning to lease land around here, live and contribute as best I can and order up something like what used to be in those snazzy trailer parks and park it and an underground bunker cut into a hillside to keep it safe from the storms. Walk out onto the level from my safe place. Heat it with a lightbulb. Feed myself with a garden growing on the roof and bring in communications that must be around. Maybe I could offer history classes, or corporate climbing to neighbours who seek something else but still want to hold on to what they have. That's my game plan."

As she listened, Emma realized how small a vision she had had. Return and look after oldsters was all she imagined. Now suddenly she had options that spread out like a prairie horizon. Günter would be the farmer he always was. He was the model of sustainability. She could drop back into a role that supported him, but she knew that the wealth at hand would allow her to realize the very dream they tried to fulfill before and failed. She could start a charitable trust and had the wherewithal to carry it out.

Mabel couldn't help but be inspired by Irene's plan. "Well, I'm a Mom for life, I think, if only by adoption. Maybe it's time to think of being so the other way." Now that she had a process to convert her treasure into something tangible, she began to wonder what she could do.

"I'm going to start a sawmill," Bill added. There is some fine lumber here that when thinned out, will let the understory grow faster. As a community, we need to catch this wave of warming climate that we're within.

*

The year following their arrival at their roots surely taxed Roger's inventiveness at coming up with plausible fantasies to explain the regular and large expenses that showed up in the accounts of Mabel, Irene, Bill, and the Werners. The items would not have been purchased by comrades in the DL community. All were covered by either allowances or Mabel's treasure and happened because of Roger's sleights of hand at the computer coding site. So, what appeared in the files as trips were really the solar arrays that appeared on local farms near the Werners. A lot of windmills pumped water into reservoirs that gravity-fed plumbing below also. Bill got a portable band saw operating.

There was a thirst for learning beyond the life skills that rural living demanded, and it went on into dark nights under artificial lighting. Being intimately familiar with simple machines, every purchaser of the newly available technology knew the handyman's translation on one of the most profound of scientific principles. In their language it was only two words - everything breaks. So as their turn came to join in the upgrading, they all bought spares and learned how to strip down things and rebuild them. Such skills had been bred into them for generations.

So it was that the arrival of a neighbour, at the gallop, that caught everyone by surprise when he drew up in Anna and Herman's yard just before the next Christmas. "The droid is gone," he reported. "The one we order all our equipment through, is gone."

Mabel immediately threw on a coat and rode with him back to the depot. They walked with caution into the square. Even from a distance, they could see something was awry. In the spot that Dent had been standing for a whole year was another droid that looked the same except it lacked the wrinkle in its dome that had given the machine its nickname to the community.

"Let's ask," Mabel said to her driver. Mabel walked to the human at the service counter and asked for her order. The person checked. "Who was it for?"

Mabel clearly gave her name and the expected result happened. The droid in Dent's spot hummed into action and approached. "How can I help to-day?" it asked with a southern nasal drawl. This voice was definitely not Dent's.

Mabel feigned surprise and looked at it critically aware that each response was likely being recorded. "I was looking for my order. Are they being sent by droid now?" she asked.

"I was sent to collect your order," the machine responded.

"Come over here," she commanded and led the way to a table away from the lineup. As she did so, the man who had driven her stepped to the desk and asked for an order.

"Not in yet," said the attendant after looking at the screen. In the chit-chat that followed before the next in line complained, the driver learned that after Mabel had sent something back to the depot last time, the one with the dented top had not returned as it always had. In its place this one had arrived and occupied the same spot.

"Well now I don't know if it is a slow delivery or the wife forgot to order it," the driver said loudly and left, looking over his shoulder at Mabel who was talking to the droid.

"I don't know what you are talking about," Mabel said imperiously to the machine. "I wanted to collect an order. I had nothing to send." She turned to step away.

The machine processed the rejection and then said to her back, "My name is Ketchup Smear and Roger Los Angeles sent me."

Every alarm bell in Mabel's being jangled. She snapped a smile back on her face and turned to face the droid.

"Now I know you are defective." She looked around and over the machine. "You don't have a smear on you, and I have no idea who Roger ... *what was the last name again* ...is."

"Los Angeles," replied the robot.

"You must have a cross-linking fault or two in your processing circuitry. Return now for repair," and she pointed to the door to the shipping area. Mabel turned with a shake of her head and headed for a different exit from the one by which she had entered. Outside, she quickly ran back to the carriage where she met the driver who had made his own way out.

"Home. I think Roger might have been busted." Mabel said. "We may have just bought our last technical upgrade."

At the Werner's she repeated every detail of the event. "Well," Irene said, "if it was too good to be true, it probably was. It's not the life I thought I had bought but ... Maybe we can reconnect later but look at the stuff we scooped anyway. Good enough is good enough, eh?"

DL INC.

DL INC.

FOR MORE TITLES BY AUTHOR K.G. WATSON PLEASE VISIT AMAZON.CA/AMAZON.COM OR YOUR NEAREST BOOKSTORE

WWW.PANDAMONIUMPUBLISHING.COM

Manufactured by Amazon.ca
Bolton, ON